CW00864142

DISCLAIMER:

"The Mystery of The Old Orphanage" is a work of fiction.
Names, characters, places and incidents are a product of the author's
imagination. Any resemblance to persons past or present is entirely
coincidental.

Copyright © Beverley Fairbanks 2020

ISBN 9-798663849-62-3

THE MYSTERY OF THE
Old Orphanage

Beverley Fairbanks

About the Author

Beverley Fairbanks was born in Nottingham in 1960, the daughter of Jamaican parents who came to Britain with the Windrush generation.

She trained as a teacher in Newcastle Upon Tyne and worked as a primary and secondary school teacher for over 34 years. In 2017, following spinal fusion she was forced to take early retirement. This gave her the opportunity to begin writing one of the many stories she created for her son Samuel – a mystery story aimed at 9–12-year-olds.

Two years later she was sadly diagnosed with Motor Neurone Disease. Illness gave her a fresh determination to do all she could to see her book in print. Finding an agent and publisher can be a slow process so, with time against her, she decided to self-publish.

Beverley has always had a fascination with old buildings and has often wondered about the tales a house could tell. The idea for "The Mystery of the Old Orphanage" came from the renovation of several old houses, but in particular her own Victorian Rectory, where she lives with her husband Dave and cockapoo Truffle.

Beverley will be donating 50% of any royalties to two charities that hold a special place in her heart, namely Motor Neurone Disease Association and Nottingham Hospice. Each of which will receive 25%!

For
Samuel Finnigan
who inspired me to write this story.

THE MYSTERY OF THE
Old Orphanage

Prologue

Kingminster 2019

The cottage was a mess, overcrowded with furniture from a bygone age. The two removal men stared in disbelief at the mixture of junk and antiques that confronted them. It was a familiar story. Someone had died and the relatives couldn't face clearing out the house, so had called in Unwin and Son's Specialist Removal team.

Climbing the dropdown ladder into the attic, Gary Unwin had to crouch in order to move in the cramped space. This was always his favourite place to start on any removal job. It was here that he would find anything of any real value which may have lain unforgotten for generations. An old packing case caught his eye. This was just the sort of place where family treasures might have been packed away and forgotten. Carefully he lifted off the dusty bed sheet that had been placed on top of the case. At first glance it appeared to contain nothing more than old birthday and anniversary cards. Sighing, Gary tossed the cards aside and looked around the densely packed space for more obvious treasures. He could see nothing of interest. Apart from a few old toys there was little else worth keeping. Turning the packing case upside down he emptied its contents onto the floor. He would put the toys in the case and leave his companion to clear the rest of what appeared to be pure junk. As the contents of the case spilled out onto the floor, Gary found himself stepping back in disbelief. A pile of old letters, very old letters some of which looked as if they had never been opened lay on the floor before him. Someone had not wanted to part with these. The stamps alone would be worth a small fortune. But it wasn't the age of the letters that had sent a shiver through his spine, but rather the name on the envelope. "Unwin", his own family name.

In his line of business Gary Unwin had come across many an interesting find, in the debris left behind once someone had died. There must be countless Unwins in Nottinghamshire. So why had this particular pile of letters set his heart racing? It was the village, Kingminster. This was the village where his family had originated many decades ago. Picking up the envelopes he slipped them into his trouser pockets. Somewhere inside his head he held a memory of stories he had heard about his Victorian relatives who had once lived in the village.

His heart was racing now, as he tried to recall the stories about the village and his family's connection to the old orphanage. Something about the letters made him feel uneasy, he felt sure he would find the answers in the letters to the questions which were now coursing through his brain. They were clearly important, and must have lain hidden in the attic for decades. Pushing the pile of letters deep into his back pocket he climbed down onto the landing below and called to his companion.

'Let's leave it for today, mate. Nothing but junk in here by the looks of it, I'll sort this lot later in the week.'

Chapter 1

The Old Rectory 2019

October 2019

The key turned easily in the lock, and Lewis entered the orphanage. It felt colder than before. The dim autumn light did little to make the place feel in any way welcoming. Switching on his torch and keeping it pointed to the floor Lewis walked into the hallway and down the second passageway to The Master's rooms. From the appearance of the room no one had been in here since September.

'Millie,' he whispered to the silent room. 'Millie can you hear me? Give me a sign,' he added.

But there was nothing. For a moment Lewis wondered at the wisdom of coming in here alone, and not leaving a note explaining where he was going. But it was too late now, he would just have to make a thorough search and then leave.

It was dark and eerily cold in The Master's bedroom. The loose floorboards creaked and screeched as he gingerly put his weight on them. Moving the rusting iron bed to one side Lewis noticed that several of the floorboards looked as if they needed nailing down. He knelt down to investigate. The boards looked as if they had never been secured to the floor. Carefully he managed to lift the nearest board. It came away easily! Pointing his torch into the void below, he could barely identify what looked like an old handkerchief made of similar fabric to the old cotton pouch that Truffle had found. He struggled to push his hand into the gap. Catching hold of a corner of the handkerchief Lewis pulled. Nothing happened, it was stuck. He realised he would have to try and take up another of the floorboards to reach it.

It was a struggle to lever out the adjoining board, for although it looked as if it too had never been nailed down, it had swollen and wedged itself firmly to the floor. Opening his school bag, Lewis found a plastic ruler. Holding it tight in the middle to ensure that it did not snap on impact, he managed to push one end of it into the gap between the boards. With a sawing action he gently moved the ruler in the gap to loosen the trapped dirt. Unfortunately, the ruler became firmly wedged and no amount of wiggling and pulling would move it. Once more he tried to lift the floorboard. At last it began to shift, snapping the ruler in two. Hastily Lewis shoved the broken pieces back into his bag and gasped at what he saw hidden under the floor.

July 2019

Three months earlier his parents' divorce had not been easy. Lewis was still reeling from the shock and how quickly the time had passed since his parents had sat him down and told him they were getting a divorce. As an only child he had no siblings with whom to discuss the impending separation and how it would impact on his life. The word itself he had heard any number of times before but had never given it much thought. Several of the children in his school came from homes where their parents had either separated or divorced, and he had taken the information as just that, information. Something he might need to know. 'A label' his mum had called it when she had been speaking to his father. He had no idea what it truly meant; no dictionary definition could describe the pain, anger and deep sadness that he had felt at the first mention of the word in connection with his life. On the plus side, if he could call it that, mum had informed him that he could have his very own dog at last. Lewis knew she had only consented to this as a bribe, and to silence his endless questions about the many changes that were taking place around him.

His home had been sold and he had been told by his parents that he and his mum would be leaving London at the end of the summer term to move to the Midlands. He had learnt through repeated questioning that they would be moving to Notting-hamshire to live in a much larger house with a huge garden. This piece of information alone had perplexed Lewis; he could not understand why he and his mother would need a larger house, and certainly not one in the country. When he had tried to question both of his parents further on the implications of the divorce, and how it would affect him, they had simultane-ously managed to find something that urgently needed their attention, rather than answer his questions. They would skirt around the topic and never gave him a direct answer. Lewis desperately wanted to know more about the plans everyone seemed to be making about his life, without once asking him what he wanted! They had always been keen to emphasise that he was a young adult when it suited them. At 12 he felt he had the right to know what his parents were planning for his future.

His mother had shown him pictures of the house that was soon to be their home. She must have taken them on her many visits to Nottingham when she had told Lewis she was on 'a course' which had clearly been a lie. The pictures of the house had done nothing to make him any happier about the move, but one picture of the village and local area had caught his eye. It was of the building he was now staring at from his new bedroom window. What was it about that redbrick Victorian monstrosity that made the hair on the back of his neck stand on end?

On a bright and cloudless July morning, Lewis and his mother had driven over 130 miles to the pretty village of Kingminster, on the edge of Nottinghamshire. Nottingham had been the birthplace of his mother, and she had settled upon it as a place to make a fresh start, without any discussion with Lewis. Nothing could have prepared him for the dusty, damp-smelling run-down former rectory that was now to be his home. Little did he know that with the help of a new friend, and a dog called Truffle he would find himself trying to solve a crime that had taken place over 150 years ago.

The Old Rectory was large and spacious. It had many rooms with high ceilings, and lots of Victorian features, some of which made Lewis feel a little uncomfortable. He liked the cast iron fireplaces in each room, although he noted that none of them looked as if they had been used in years. The kitchen and a room called a scullery were old fashioned and gloomy with a large black iron range cooker. The whole house was sorely in need of modernisation, though even Lewis could appreciate its old-world charm.

He had been able to choose his own bedroom and had selected one of the large rooms at the front of the house overlooking a field full of sheep. Next to the fireplace stood an enormous oak wardrobe. It must have been built in the room itself, as it could not have fitted through the door or even the window. His mother had the room opposite also at the front of the house. There were two more bedrooms on the first floor, both of which were also spacious, bright and airy.

Looking out of his new bedroom window Lewis surveyed the view. In the foreground was an idyllic country scene, a field full of grazing sheep, hedges, a small stream and distant woodlands. But within this picture postcard image was something altogether more sinister and disconcerting. At a distance of approximately 400 metres stood a large imposing Victorian building. Something about it made him feel uneasy. He had earlier learnt that the building had previously been known as 'Eden Orphanage'. It held secrets of that he was sure. No building could have stood for so long without having a past. For some reason Lewis felt that the past for this particular building would not be pleasant. The emotions it evoked were difficult for him to understand. The building itself was impressive architecturally. But somehow Lewis got the feeling that something cruel and ugly had taken place within its walls.

The feeling that Eden Orphanage was somehow watching him and at the same time daring him to come closer and take a look was very strong. What was it about the redbrick Victorian monstrosity that made the hair on the back of his neck stand on end? As he stared at the building Lewis reflected that perhaps divorce and moving to a new house wasn't so bad, compared with living in an orphanage with no parents at all. Downstairs he could hear his mother's voice becoming more agitated and shrill, as she directed the removal men who were unloading their lives from the back of a van.

'How had it come to this?' mused Lewis. 'We were happy living in London, at least I was.'

It would be some time later that Lewis would discover the reason for the house's decline. Over the years the Rectors had all complained of strange noises and unexplained draughts.

Doors that opened and closed by themselves. Added to which were reports that the Rectory itself seemed to be sad! The locals told tales of a young girl haunting the upstairs rooms and garden. Eventually a new building had been found for the Rectory on the other side of the village. The original Rectory had been put up for sale as a family home. However, attempts to sell the house had always resulted in it being put straight back on the market. There were reports of strange movements and unexplained noises night and day. Lewis's mum had heard nothing of the Rectory's history. In her haste to find a new home for herself and her son, she had marvelled at its low price, and had snapped it up after one viewing.

Mum had explained that she planned to use one of the bedrooms as an office and might consider letting Lewis have one of the attic rooms at the top of the house as his games room. The idea of having a games room had cheered Lewis up a little, but when he went to explore the attic rooms his spirits fell.

Climbing the steep stairs Lewis found himself on a narrow landing. The aged bare pine floorboards creaked noisily, and even though Lewis knew he wasn't doing anything wrong he got the distinct expression that the floorboards were giving out a warning. Warning him in some way, but of what he had no idea. Two doors led off the corridor, the first led to a small box room, with a dusty skylight window covered in bird droppings on the outside and cobwebs on the inside. Lewis quickly closed the door and headed towards the door at the end of the landing. If his bearings were correct, he would be at the back of the house over the kitchen/scullery. This door had been shaped to accommodate the sloping ceiling and led into another bedroom.

Considering the size of the main bedrooms on the landing below, this room was small and pokey. At the back of the house it faced north, so was cooler than Lewis's south facing front bedroom. But even the drop in temperature couldn't explain the feeling of despair and sadness within it. Something bad had happened in here. Lewis felt as though the room itself or a presence was trying to talk to him. Goosebumps covered his body as he stepped over to the narrow sash window. To tell the truth, Lewis had wanted to turn and run the moment he had opened the door to the larger of the attic bedrooms. He felt that as he breathed in the stale air of the room something not from this world had entered his body. The rusting cast iron fireplace fanned cold air into the room on this hot July day, and the grate had signs of even more bird droppings mingled with specks of soot. But it wasn't the dirt or even the dark cramped space that had unnerved Lewis, it was a feeling that the room had a secret and wanted to share it with him. The feeling was akin to being in a crowded room with everyone trying to catch your attention at the same time, he could swear he heard voices anxiously shouting in his head, but what they were saying he had no idea. Lewis's emotions were too raw from the divorce, the move and having to leave his dad and friends. Pulling the door firmly shut behind him he left the room.

'Later,' he whispered as he hurried down the stairs and shut himself in his bedroom.

Even with the packing cases waiting to be unpacked and none of his computer games, or 'toys' as mum called them ready to be used, this room felt safe and comfortable. Not being a coward was something that Lewis prided himself on. He knew he would never sleep easily until he was able to brave another visit to the attic room, and try to find the source of the despair, if that were at all possible.

It took several minutes for Lewis to feel he could face his mother and appear normal. Mum had taken to scrutinising his face for signs of tears and sadness. She was obviously feeling very guilty about the divorce, uprooting Lewis and moving him so far away from his father. Lewis in turn didn't want to upset his mother; he had heard her crying in the night before they had finally left London. Dad had told him that he was now the man of the house, and that he must try to look after mum. Lewis certainly didn't want to make mum cry or upset her by telling her about the bad feelings he had experienced in the attic bedroom.

'Why are the attic are rooms so small and dark Mum?' he asked in what sounded like a squeaky voice.

Mum looked up from the packing case she was unpacking and stared hard at her son.

'What's up Mr Woo?' she asked, using her pet name for him. He knew that she had sensed that something had disturbed him.

'Oh, I was just exploring, and was surprised at how pokey and dark the two rooms are,' he replied trying to make his voice sound normal and give the impression that he didn't really care.

Mum knowing her son well, decided to let it go for now. Instead she went on to explain that the rooms would have been the servants' bedrooms. In digesting this piece of information Lewis formed the opinion that the Victorians didn't much care for the welfare of their servants. Perhaps this was what had caused him to feel uneasy in the attic rooms, but the voices he couldn't explain. He wondered how he would have felt to have lived in the Victorian Era and be part of this house. After all, although the house was in dire need of modernisation it was nevertheless very grand, yet the spaces formerly occupied by the servants were nothing more than functional. In an attempt to shake off the feeling of gloom Lewis decided to explore the garden.

Stepping outside through the room mum had told him used

to be a scullery, Lewis noticed two doors leading into what he assumed were old fashioned outhouses. The first door opened inwards into what had once been the old coal house. It was a damp, dark and airless room with no window, but then again why would a place used to store coal need a window? It now held an old oil boiler, presumably for the central heating. There was coal dust on the floor and in every corner. The room looked as though it hadn't been used for years. After a cursory glance to his right and left Lewis decided it could stay unexplored and moved onto the next door. Now this was most certainly something from the past. It held an ugly Victoria toilet, complete with a rotting wooden seat and high-level cistern. Out of curiosity Lewis pulled the chain and the toilet actually flushed.

'Useful I suppose,' he muttered, as he closed the door and stood on the patio.

The large garden was a young person's dream. There was an orchard and numerous trees Lewis had never seen. Despite being in need of several weeks' worth of weeding, Lewis could appreciate that this too had once been a beautiful and well-tended space. He knew where he would be spending most of the summer holidays. The trees begged to be climbed, Lewis smiled to himself as he imagined himself playing with his very own dog. Perhaps living in the countryside might not be so bad after all, he thought.

'And as long as I don't have to go into that attic room again,' he added aloud, as if to cement that thought as a certainty.

But saying it was one thing, Lewis knew he would have to visit the attic bedroom again in order to feel comfortable about living and indeed sleeping in The Old Rectory.

The rest of day passed uneventfully, and soon beds were made and mum had produced a meal consisting of bread, boiled eggs and cheese. Lewis was aware that his mother kept glancing at him as they sat at the kitchen table eating and discussing plans for the house.

'What say we get a notebook and go around the house and decide on what needs to be done?' she suggested.

'That will take all night,' replied Lewis, not looking up from his plate.

He most certainly didn't want to go anywhere near the attic again that day, and most definitely not before he was about to go to bed and try to sleep in this strange house. But he didn't want mum to know this and he remembered dad's words, about being the man of the house, so he swallowed his food and gave his mum a weak smile.

'Let's start downstairs and leave upstairs until another day,' he suggested trying to make light of the situation.

Mum had guessed that something was wrong. She knew that his mood had changed after he had visited the attic rooms. She wondered whether he was simply sensitive about the contrast in living conditions of the Victorians and their servants. Lewis had always hated the idea that people could be used as servants and ill-treated just because they were poor. When they had studied the Victorian Era at school, Lewis had frequently come home from school enraged about the differences in lifestyles between rich and poor. And now here he was living in the house of what would have been a fairly well-off Victorian Rector. Granted it was run down, but the stark differences between master and servant were clear to be seen throughout the house in its layout and construction.

Sensing that Lewis was unwilling to help with her list of improvements mum decided to leave the list making until another day. Both were exhausted, and so an early night was suggested. After a soak in a large cast iron bath (there was no shower), Lewis sat his computer table and turned on his laptop. Thankfully mum had insisted they were connected to the internet prior to the move. As she had expected Lewis had connected his laptop to the internet as his first priority. He decided to send his old school friends in London a quick message along with photos he had taken with his phone as he explored the house. The removal men had placed his computer desk in front of the window, which gave him a beautiful view of the grazing sheep, stream and woodland. The only other building on the horizon was the large and imposing Eden Orphanage. It looked like something out of a horror film, sinister and definitely frightening. Not the sort of place that any orphaned child would wish to live in. Perhaps it was the boarded-up windows on the ground floor, which added to the look of desolation. He decided he would search the internet for information on the village of Kingminster, which was now to be his home. He particularly wanted to find out more about the history of the orphanage. Despite being some 400 metres from his new home, Lewis felt that someone or something was watching him from behind one of the large stained windows on the upper two floors. The feeling it gave him was akin to what he had felt when he had first explored the attic rooms. If he could have put it into words, he would have said that something very sad and cruel linked the two places.

Chapter 2

Millie and James 1860

Eden Orphanage stood proud and imposing eight miles from Nottingham town, in the picturesque village of Kingminster. It had been named after its founder Joshua Eden, a rich and powerful philanthropist who had made his money in the thriving textile industry. He had commissioned the construction of the orphanage several years earlier and had insisted that it was built not in Nottingham town itself, but rather on his own land. In endowing the orphanage, Joshua had hoped his legacy would guarantee his place in history. He had also made it very clear to the staff that he wished to be involved in the day to day running of the place. Its close proximity to his own home Eden Manor meant that he could drop in at any time he chose. The local people considered him a kind and charitable benefactor, which indeed he was, but sadly Joshua Eden had chosen the wrong people to aid him in his quest to help the poor children of Nottinghamshire.

For Millie and James Cooper, it was now their home. Brother and younger sister had lost both parents to cholera in January of that year. James who was 14 and Millie who was twelve, had been given no choice regarding where they were to live or how they would survive. So it was that the church had stepped in and placed the two siblings in Eden Orphanage. 'Workhouse' would have been a more accurate description of the place. Education was sparse and work plentiful. The children rose early and spent the days assigned to menial and often back breaking tasks. For James the move to the orphanage had proved to be a bit of a mixed blessing. He was glad that he still had Millie with him. He had worried that they might have been split up on the death of their parents. James still held his dream, that one day he and Millie would be able to leave the orphanage and start to live their lives their own way.

Life in the orphanage wasn't all bad for Millie. Like all of the children she too had to work hard, cleaning and polishing as well as washing and ironing. However, one of her many duties was to clean Mr Eden's study in the orphanage. For the first time in her life Millie had the opportunity to handle many fascinating books. Hers was a bright inquiring mind but due to birth she had been destined for a life of servitude. If she been born today, she would have been a challenge for Joshua Eden and his business empire. Although she could barely read, the many books she had to dust weekly seemed to draw her into their magical and mysterious world. They cast a spell over her. She would often imagine herself travelling to faraway places where exotic animals lived, and the sun shone every day. She would gently turn the pages and gaze in amazement at the sketches of animals and plants she had never heard of. Thankfully for our little heroine life was soon to change. Millie was fortunate enough to catch the eye of the local Reverend's wife, Cynthia Peabody.

Mrs Peabody had taken up residence as the Reverend's wife two years prior to the start of our story. She was beautiful, and full of fun, and loved the company of young people. Bored with the endless morning visits and tea drinking which seemed to be her main duties as wife to the Reverend, Cynthia had volunteered to teach a few classes at the orphanage. A number of the brighter girls had been selected for the classes. Millie had been desperate to be one of the selected few and had been overcome with joy when she had been told she was to join the group. The time spent in the school room with the fragrant and witty Mrs Peabody was the best part of her week. Unlike some of the other girls, she did not see the lessons as a time to relax and escape the daily grind of housework. Admittedly she enjoyed being allowed to sit and rest her aching limbs, but best of all was the chance to devour the selection of books Cynthia had assembled for the girls to use in their studies. Millie would often ask questions about the characters and places she read about in the much-thumbed books, showing a greater level of interest in their studies than any of the other girls in the class. Cynthia liked the tall skinny curly-haired girl and felt that here was one poor mite she could possibly save. She formulated her plan and decided on the best approach to put the idea into her husband's head. One evening after a hearty meal, Cynthia felt that the time was right. They had left the dining room and had moved into their comfortable parlour. The Reverend Peabody sat in his favourite armchair reading '*The Nottingham Journal*'.

'I need another maid darling,' she muttered as she poured her husband a cup of tea.

'What's that my dear?' replied her husband, barely lifting his head from the newspaper he was so engrossed in.

'I say my dear, looks like the police are no closer to catching the burglars,' commented Archibald Peabody, as he squinted at the newspaper in his lap. The burglars he was referring to had been responsible for a spate of crimes, specifically targeting the larger and wealthier homes of the residents of Kingminster and district.

'Do I have your permission to choose a new maid?

Obviously, I wouldn't dream of getting rid of Agnes. But she is rather slow witted and quick to take offence,' she added in an attempt to convince her husband of the need for change.

Agnes Grimes was indeed slow witted and very surly. The Reverend and his wife had simply inherited her along with the job and the Rectory. Agnes aged 15, had come from a long line of Grimes's who served the Eden estate.

'Have you anyone in mind?' asked her husband. A frown had now set firmly on his face, the one she often saw when he had to discuss or confront matters of money.

'I was thinking of one of the girls from the orphanage, her name is Millie Cooper. She's bright, keen and strong. I think she would make an excellent maid and wouldn't cost us a penny,' added Cynthia with a twinkle in her eye.

She knew that a free servant would be something her husband might agree to, and it would give him material that he could use in one of his many sermons on helping the poor!

The plan worked, and within the space of a week, Millie had left the orphanage and moved the short distance to The Rectory. The move for Millie had not been as sad as she had thought, once she realised she would still be on Joshua Eden's land and able to see James each week when she would attend Cynthia's classes at the orphanage. Both brother and sister had been relieved that one of them would be free from the harsh regime of The Master.

The smell of rotting horse manure, the flies and dirt, along with the effort needed to work on an almost empty stomach always made James feel lightheaded. His fellow work mate and young friend George had just been sick behind the barn. Today George would have been called delicate, but in the world of the orphanage Master, Mike Unwin, he was considered a malingerer, workshy and downright lazy. James recognised George's weak constitution and knew that the lad would never grow up to be a man. James had watched his own father struggle with life, and at times been too ill to eat or drink. George also knew that his only hope of a better life was to leave the orphanage. James was glad that his little sister had escaped the drudgery of life in the orphanage.

'The Rectory can't be worse than this place,' James had told George, when hearing George boast of his big plans to become rich in London.

George had heard some of the older boys talking of breaking out of the orphanage and running away. Not being very bright George had thought this a brilliant plan. He had boasted to James as they lay in their iron beds at night, that he would go to London and become rich. He would then come back to Kingminster and beat The Master and his staff to a pulp. Fighting talk, yes and it helped to keep him going. Sadly, history has taught us that such plans need a little more detail in order to succeed. James hadn't the heart to tell George he thought his plans were half baked. Which is a pity really because it could have saved a lot of people a lot of trouble and grief.

This particular muck shovelling day was to be no ordinary day. As usual the work was hard, the staff cruel and the food even crueller, but neither James nor George would have thought it would have ended as it did.

Chapter 3

A Robbery Takes Place 1860

On a clear June evening in 1860 events at the orphanage were to change, and for some the consequences would be felt for decades. George and his group of friends had spent days and weeks talking and dreaming of a better life in London. None knew where London was or why it would have been any better than Nottingham, but it was the capital city and that was good enough for them. How to get to it was an incidental matter that they would address once they had broken out of the orphanage. The boys were desperate to leave. They had received very little education other than how to work the land. All dreamt of a life which did not involve drudgery. Fuelled with the growing desire to be free from servitude the boys made the decision that tonight would be the night that they leave Eden Orphanage for good. However, unknown to George and his friends a robbery was to take place that same evening only half a mile away, at the home of none other than Joshua Eden.

The orphanage was managed by an outwardly charming man called Mike Unwin, otherwise known to the staff and children as The Master. He hired and fired the staff and was at the epicentre of all things pertaining to the building. Nothing happened within its walls without the knowledge of The Master. He ensured that the children were poorly fed, inadequately clothed and forced to work ridiculously long hours. Michael Unwin was tall, lean and had a handsome face. To all who did not cross him, he was a pleasant man. He had secured his place at the orphanage by ingratiating himself with Joshua Eden, a few years prior to the start of this story, at a time when the great man had suffered a personal crisis. His elevation from clerk in Eden's lace factory, to Master of the orphanage, had done little to satisfy his greed and yearning for money. He would closely watch his employer in an attempt to emulate his gestures and mannerisms. Mike Unwin was learning how to be a gentleman. The practical side of his plan had been in operation for several years. He would soon have enough money to move on, but for now the orphanage would be his home. Mike Unwin considered himself to be more than a member of staff in the orphanage. To this end he had refused to sleep in one of the second-floor rooms, where the staff had their rooms. Instead he had secured two rooms on the ground floor as his own, and apart from supervising any staff member who entered them, he kept his own council and company.

Mike Unwin had learnt from an early age that a person could project many faces, and it was vital to select the correct face for a particular situation. Those that worked with him thought him hard and cruel but believed that these traits were part of his job description. Charm he had in abundance which he could turn on as if flicking a switch when he thought it necessary. However, he also had another more sinister side, which few people had ever seen. In short he was totally dishonest and without scruples. Possibly a life of hard knocks had helped to shape him into the unfeeling person that he had become, but despite appearing caring, conscientious and considerate to his employer, Mike Unwin served only one master and that was himself.

He would scrutinize the boys and some of the girls on arrival at the orphanage, looking for similar personality traits to his own. These children would be tested for their loyalty to him before being put to meaningful work which would line his pockets and those of his Nottingham associates. He had passed over James, Millie and George for several reasons. James was far too honest and keen to look after his little sister. Boys who cared for others were of no use to him, although the sister could always be used as leverage with The Law if it became necessary. In George's case he was too weak and sickly, a bit of pressure from the local constabulary would have him singing like a canary! The sort of person that Mike Unwin favoured needed to be fit, free of morals and willing to do his bidding without asking any questions. These were the children, mainly boys, whom he could groom and initiate in the art of theft. The boys were often slight which was useful for breaking into houses through small windows often left unchecked at the back of a house. Through careful tuition they had learnt how to spot a genuine item of jewellery from costume jewellery made from paste.

Joshua Eden's desire to be fully involved in the operation of his orphanage from the start had meant that a number of rooms had been set aside for his personal use when he was in the building. These consisted of a sitting room, study and private toilet, all situated on the ground floor. Unbeknown to Mr Eden, Mike Unwin would in his absence use the rooms to practise for his future life as a gentleman. Mike Unwin took great pleasure in striding from room to room with his head held high and his shoulders back, practising his speech and trying hard to lose his Nottinghamshire accent.

In early 1860 several of the finer houses in the neighbourhood of Kingminster and district experienced a number of burglaries, in which mainly jewellery had been stolen. One of the few grand houses that had not been targeted had been that of Joshua Eden. To put things right and to throw suspicion off himself and his boys The Master had decided that it was time to steal from his employer: the timing was right. The previous week he had overheard Mr Eden and the Rector's wife discussing a trip he and his family would be making to Nottingham town on the coming Monday. Joshua Eden had told Cynthia Peabody that they would be staying overnight in Nottingham, as he had business matters that required his attention. Mike had been glad to hear that the great man would not be at home when his house was burgled. To give him his due it was a task he did not relish. If a mistake was made, he knew he would most probably hang.

Now Joshua Eden, while having a kind and generous heart, was also a vain and pompous man. He loved to show off his wealth in every aspect of his life. His clothes were elegant and made of the finest fabrics and adorned with beautiful Nottingham lace from his very own factory in the town, as were those of his wife and only surviving daughter Annabel. Both women were seldom seen without conspicuous amounts of jewellery. The orphanage was just another means of displaying his wealth, and to ensure he would be remembered as an eminent philanthropist. He had built and opened the orphanage as both a good deed and in order to curry favour with The Great and The Good. He hoped that his name might one day reach the ear of the Queen. He longed to be remembered and revered in the history books that were already being written charting the marvels of the Victorian Era. To this end he had commissioned numerous family portraits of himself with his wife and remaing daughter Annabel, each depicting his grand status. Eden Manor was a fine and impressive building and one which spoke volumes of its owner's wealth.

The local burglaries had baffled the newly formed police force. It was clear that the crimes were being committed by a well organised gang, who had to have local knowledge of the properties that had been targeted to date. Who they were and how to catch them was another matter. Known criminals were also beginning to wonder and marvel at who was responsible for their discomfort. Most were becoming tired and somewhat annoyed at having to produce an alibi each time one of the larger houses was burgled.

As the Master of a large charitable institution, Mike Unwin was in the privileged position of securing employment for his young charges when they reached 17 or sometimes earlier. In its short existence the orphanage had managed to place several of the older boys and girls into domestic service within the Nottinghamshire area. Once in their new position, as a show of care and wellbeing The Master would visit his recent charges. This gave him an opportunity to assess the layout of the house and decide whether it was worth a visit from his lads. Even better if the young person was dishonest, and willing to provide him with detailed information on how the household was run. He had widened his circle of crime, and now had men, boys and girls in Nottingham town itself. They were able to provide transport to and from planned burglaries where necessary.

After a successful night's work, Mike would take the stolen items to an associate in Nottingham town, who was himself a jeweller. The more valuable items of jewellery were usually broken down then taken to London where they would be reset and made up into entirely different pieces from the original. These were then sold on, with a large share of the profit entering the pockets of The Master. The orphan boys received no payment but rather privileges of easier work, better food and more free time. It would not do for an orphan boy to have cash about his person!

On that fateful day in June, James and George had moved

from spreading manure, and were now cutting the long grass which would be stored for animal feed in the winter. By the end of the working day the sun was setting, and the air was cooling. The boys were hungry for their evening meal. Both were hot, tired and exhausted from a hard day working in the burning June sun, and were glad of a chance to rest in their gloomy dormitory. The customary practice was for the children to listen to a reading from the Bible followed by prayer, before going to sleep. However, given that the majority of the staff and children could barely read or write their own names, not a lot of Bible reading took place.

Tom, a former workhouse boy, had been pleased at the chance of employment at the orphanage. Part of his many duties was to supervise the boys as they prepared for bed. He had now reached the grand age of 22, and was grateful to The Master and Joshua Eden for their charity. He had received a sparse education which consisted mainly of learning by repetition The Lord's Prayer and The Ten Commandments, but he had still to master the art of reading and writing. An understanding existed between Tom and the boys, which allowed the boys their only chance of freedom from the strict discipline of the orphanage. As long as they kept their voices low, they could converse with one another freely. If The Master were to appear, all would immediately jump up from their beds, kneel, and begin to recite The Lord's Prayer.

That evening the boys lay on top of their thin blankets and whispered to one another in the stifling heat of the stuffy room. George had followed a group of boys into a corner where they were deep in conversation. Something was being planned, but what it was James didn't care or want to know. He was however concerned that the naïve George might find himself in more trouble than he could handle. James gave little thought to what George and his friends might be discussing, but before falling into a deep sleep he decided he needed to keep an eye on George and hopefully steer him in the right direction.

All was silent apart from the gentle snoring of the boys, and the scratching of rats. A sudden unusual noise woke James from his slumber. It was the sound of boys walking on the tips of their toes and trying not to breathe too loudly. James heard George's iron bed creak as he too got up.

'What are you doing George?' he whispered.

'Go back to sleep,' replied George excitedly. 'I'm leaving, me and the boys are leaving this place for good.'

In the dark stuffy dormitory James was unable to see what was happening. The room was pitch black. For a moment he did wonder how the boys were going to escape from the locked dormitory. Suddenly there was a loud crash, and the sound of splintering wood. One of the boys had been too forceful in breaking the lock on the door, the noise woke the whole dormitory. All quickly understood what was taking place and decided to help in any way they could. Unfortunately, the noise had also carried downstairs. Tom who was particularly nosy had been lingering outside Joshua Eden's study door curious as to what The Master might be doing in there alone. At the sound of the dormitory door been forced open he immediately rushed back upstairs shouting to alert the other members of staff that something was afoot.

Now while the boys were making their bid for freedom a successful robbery had just taken place only half a mile away at Eden Manor. Mike Unwin had carefully chosen this evening to have his employer's house burgled, knowing that on such occasions Joshua Eden would leave him the key to his study in the orphanage, in which was kept a strong box containing cash for staff wages and other incidental items. It was a fine hot June evening, which in his opinion was even better for the robbery. A maid might accidentally leave a downstairs window open and apart from the staff the house would be empty.

His lads, now well practised in breaking and entering a locked house, had on this occasion escaped with a sizable horde of jewellery and trinkets. Both mother and daughter had left the bulk of their fine jewellery at home. A short trip to Nottingham town and an overnight stay with other factory owners had not warranted impressive items of adornment. If all went to plan the break-in would not be discovered until the following morning.

On a 'normal' job, the stolen items were usually left outside Joshua Eden's study window hidden at the base of a large rhododendron bush which grew close to the orphanage. Prior to any robbery taking place, a number of boys would find themselves in deep trouble with The Master. They would be told that they would have to work through the night to make up for their lax attitude to their daily tasks. This was all a show, and to account for any empty beds in the boys dormitory. The 'night work force' would be supervised by The Master himself. None of the staff had shown any inclination to be involved in the discipline of the disobedient boys. All would avoid The Master, in the hope that he might not decide to pass on this extra work to them! The boys were supposedly locked in the workroom and made to work in total silence. Mike Unwin could often be heard shouting and even thrashing the workforce. If any staff member were unfortunate enough to pass him in the corridor outside the workroom, his face alone was enough for them to bow their head and move swiftly along. Once the boys had sneaked back into the orphanage, through a window deliberately left open by Mike Unwin, they would wait in the scullery for him to escort them upstairs to their dormitory. But first he must make his rounds of the building. Any of the staff who saw him would assume that he was simply ensuring that all was safe and that he was inspecting the windows from the outside to ensure none had been left open.

Mike Unwin would then walk around the building making his inspection as was normal. On reaching the study window he would bend down using the bush to screen his movements and pretend to be adjusting his shoes. He would then quickly slip the cotton pouches containing the stolen jewels into his pockets.

On this June evening all was to go horribly wrong. With Joshua Eden away, The Master decided to enjoy his freedom and treat himself to a glass of Mr Eden's fine whisky and smoke one of his employer's many cigars while he waited for his boys to return. It felt good sitting in Joshua Eden's high-backed leather chair leisurely smoking the cigar and sipping a glass of whisky.

'This is more like it,' he murmured to himself, as the warmth of the whisky mellowed his mood, and his head began to nod, but his feelings of benevolence were to be short lived.

Upstairs in the dormitories the candles had been extinguished and the children, tired out from a long day of servitude, would soon be fast asleep. The staff would also be settling down for a good night's rest, if not gambling or playing cards in the downstairs back room which served as a dining room cum rest room for them.

Poor George and his three friends had no idea that this of all nights was to be the worst night to make their dash for freedom. The boys had earlier formulated their simple plan of waiting for Tom who supervised their dormitory to leave and lock the door. Having listened carefully to his movements on numerous other occasions they knew his familiar tread on the stairs as he went downstairs to join the rest of the staff before going to bed. They had decided when all was quiet and the other boys fast asleep they would make their move. They planned to break out of the orphanage either through the front door, or a window. Further than that they had no definite plan.

They were simply desperate to leave the orphanage. They hadn't considered what might happen if they were caught, or even if they were successful and got away. It was escape by any means. Thankfully, for the little band of escapees, the other inhabitants of the dormitory had collectively realised the situation on hearing the dormitory door being forced open. All had helped to cause the confusion which had allowed George and his three friends to quietly slip down the stairs and hide themselves in a broom cupboard under the stairs. Mike Unwin had also heard the unusual noise coming from what sounded like the boys' dormitory, and had rushed from the study, only seconds after George and his friends had pulled shut the door of the broom cupboard.

The heat in the cupboard was stifling, added to this was the smell of four sweaty boys. Ned, the eldest boy, gingerly opened the door and scanned the hall for an escape route. He saw the locked and bolted front door, and several other closed doors and one standing wide open. Quickly whispering to the other boys Ned explained what he had seen through the crack in the door. On his word they were all to run as fast as they could towards the open door, make for the window and escape through that. All held their breath, while summoning up the courage to leave the safety of the broom cupboard and risk being caught. Each boy knew that if they didn't make it out of the orphanage by way of the room's window, their lives would be over. Children who had attempted to run away in the past had been so severely beaten that they were never the same again. Collectively all knew that the open door to whichever room it led into was their only way out. They had got this far and if the window was unlocked or better still open (after all it was a very warm evening) they would be free. They were so fuelled by adrenaline that each felt certain that a locked window would be no deterrent to their escape. Their yearning for freedom was so great, all knew this was their one chance. They had to make a break from the cover of the broom cupboard and head for the open door, smash the window if need be and climb out. As one they held their breath as Ned gently eased open the cupboard door; the sound of the commotion upstairs could be heard all too clearly. The Master's booming voice made each boy wince in turn at the thought of the beating they would receive if they didn't manage to escape immediately. Ned signalled with his hand for the boys to move, and as one they ran towards the open door.

Fortunately for the boys the bottom section of the window had been pushed up to allow cool air to circulate in the warm room. Taking full advantage of their good fortune each took it in turn to jump out of the open window. But as George jumped, he landed awkwardly, something hard had caught his left foot and caused him to twist his ankle. There was no time to investigate what he had landed on. Stifling a cry of pain he got up immediately, but not before reaching down to pick up the sharp object lying under the rhododendron bush that he had landed on. Stuffing what at first glance looked like an old handkerchief full of rocks into his pocket he hobbled after the other boys.

Chapter 4
A Puppy 2019

Lewis woke to bird song and no other sounds. It was early, the sun was coming up. He was gradually getting used to the silence that came with living in the country. It had now been a week since they had moved into the run-down Old Rectory. Looking at his phone he noted that the time was 05:05am and here he was again making yet another early start to another uneventful day. He reasoned that it must be the light that was brighter in the countryside in the mornings. Having lived all his life in London he was accustomed to the sound of traffic, and the hustle and bustle of people on the go night and day. He had never really noticed the sunlight and its intensity until now. Getting up, he tip-toed across to his mum's bedroom and listened at the door. He could hear her gently snoring, so decided not to wake her. Instead he went back into his bedroom and pulled open the curtains. Bright sunlight flooded the room.

Scanning the horizon, he at first saw nothing of any interest. Then he spotted it, a white van parked on Kingminster Lane, fifty metres or so down from the deserted orphanage. The van was partially hidden in a clearing under a large copper beech tree. Someone had just opened the driver's door, and then changed their mind and closed it again. That in itself should not have aroused suspicion. He or she might have broken down or be taking a call. Thinking no more of it Lewis opened his laptop and logged onto the internet. He wanted to find out a little more about the ugly monstrosity that had once been an orphanage. His search told him that it was now owned by Addbridge Construction Ltd, a large multi-national company that specialised in luxury hotels. The building was clearly empty and by the look of it in a very sorry state. Addbridge Construction Ltd would have to spend a great deal of money to turn that ugly pile into a luxury hotel thought Lewis, as he looked again at the imposing red brick Victorian orphanage. Even the bright sunlight seemed to evade the enormous building. It was as if it were permanently cast in a shadow.

Opening his laptop Lewis began messaging his friends in London. He decided to add a photo of the view from his bedroom window. He wanted them to feel a connection to his new home. He had promised to send them a daily selection of photos of the house and surrounding area. Picking up his mobile phone and approaching the window Lewis was in time to see a tall slim man stepping from the driver's door of the van. The man glanced furtively around, as if making sure no one was watching and walked quickly towards the deserted orphanage. At that moment he stared across at the houses on Church Lane and seemed to look directly at Lewis. Lewis instantly ducked down from the window, he was still holding his phone and his heart was now racing. Something about the way in which the man had looked around had told him that this was someone who didn't want to be seen.

Slowly easing himself up and using the open curtain as a shield Lewis looked from right to left for the man. He spotted him at the closed iron gates of the orphanage. He now had his back to Lewis and seemed to be wrestling with something at the gates.

'A lock perhaps?' whispered Lewis to himself.

Holding his phone up at the window he quickly took three successive shots of the mystery man. He then aimed the camera at the van, and although it was partially obscured by the large copper beech tree and some distance away, he again took another three shots of the van. He decided to remain concealed by his bedroom curtain and watch. Something sinister was definitely afoot. White van man seemed unable to perform the task of opening the gate without checking he wasn't being observed. Worse for Lewis was the fact that each time the man turned he appeared to stare directly across at him in his hiding place behind the bedroom curtains. What seemed like an hour passed as Lewis watched the man struggle to open one of large wrought iron gates.

Even at a distance of some 400 metres, Lewis imagined he could hear the faint scraping of the iron gate as it was pushed open. White van man appeared to be on high alert now. He had bent forward and hunched his body as if to make himself smaller and less obvious. He was ever watchful, glancing all around and at the house next door to make sure no one had heard or seen him open the gates. From his vantage point behind the curtain Lewis had a good side-on view of the drive leading up to the front entrance of the orphanage. He focused his eyes on the front door fully expecting the man to be heading in this direction, but he was wrong. Instead the man disappeared from view heading for what Lewis assumed was the rear of the building. After watching and waiting for several minutes Lewis gave up and made up his mind to explore his new home afresh. Perhaps the attic rooms would be brighter and more homely in the sunlight. Not wishing to frighten his mother Lewis once again listened outside her bedroom door before he made his way to the stairs leading up to the attic.

The uncarpeted rough pine stairs were cold beneath his bare feet, as he silently climbed to the attic bedrooms. He decided that the smaller box room wasn't worth his time. It was uninteresting and although he guessed at one time it might have been a bedroom, it remained a soulless and empty space. His interest was in the larger of the two rooms: the room overlooking the back garden, the outside toilet and coal house. This had been the room that had frightened him on his first visit a week ago. He had not been up to the room since that first day, and he had tried to block it out of his thoughts whenever he was on the first-floor landing. However, he was determined that if he was to be happy in this old house he needed to feel at ease in every room. He reassured himself that his first impression had been nothing more than sadness at leaving his beautiful home in London.

For some reason he had found himself dreaming of ghosts, almost on a nightly basis since he had moved into The Old Rectory. This had made him feel uncomfortable about the creepy attic room. In an attempt to conquer his dislike of the room, he knew he needed to face his fear head on. Dad had always told him that ghosts did exist, and most were friendly lost spirits trying to find their way out of this world into the next. Like spiders they were part of life and shouldn't be feared. Fine talk at the time, but Lewis didn't feel quite so confident now as he tentatively pushed open the door to the larger of the attic rooms. A blast of cold air hit him. It almost felt like someone had breathed ice cold air into his face.

'Pull yourself together Lewis,' he told himself. 'The room is empty.'

The room was indeed empty. The rusting fireplace with the bird droppings looked back at him like a wide gaping mouth. Stepping over to the window Lewis looked out across the garden. Below was the moss stained roof of the old coal house. Even on this bright summer morning the room was unnaturally cold. The bare floorboards creaked as he walked around the perimeter of the small room. There it was again - that cold air! It seemed to come from behind him now, as if someone were standing close to his left shoulder and breathing heavily. Lewis held his breath and listened; he was convinced he could almost hear someone breathing deeply. He turned suddenly but there was nothing there, just the sloping ceiling and the cut-away door. Hurriedly leaving the room, Lewis had to stop himself from running down the stairs.

'Ghosts can't hurt you; ghosts can't hurt you; ghosts can't hurt you,' he chanted in the form of a mantra as he forced himself to walk slowly down the steep stairs.

'Mr Woo!'

If it were really possible for a person to jump out of their skin, Lewis would have done so at that moment. Mum was standing on the landing below, a look of confusion on her face as she stared at her son. Lewis looked agitated and frightened as he took the stairs two at a time.

'What's up? Have you been exploring again?' she asked looking hard into his face.

'Yeah, just couldn't sleep and thought I'd have a look at the garden from the attic,'

Mum shook her head, as she often did when she was trying to read Lewis's thoughts.

'Why don't you get washed and dressed and I'll make breakfast.'

With that she turned and walked back into her bedroom. The move to The Old Rectory was clearly spooking Lewis. She had heard his chanting as he descended the attic stairs. Perhaps a visit to Mrs Featherstone, the dog breeder and her puppies would help to lift his spirits.

Once in his bedroom, Lewis realised he had been holding his breath. Breathing normally, he tried to make sense of the strange feeling he had experienced in the attic bedroom. Never having been in the presence of a ghost before, Lewis couldn't say what had caused the drop in temperature, or the impression that something or someone unseen had been present in the room. He told himself that it was his imagination getting the better of him. It was because the house was old and run down. Dad used to say that a lick of paint could make even the dullest room seem bright. Perhaps if he suggested to mum that she decorate the room it might not feel quite so spooky! But he didn't really believe this. Something wasn't right, he just knew it. Glancing out of the window towards the old orphanage he noted that the white van had gone and so, presumably, had the man. For a quiet country village this place was certainly not so quiet, he thought, as he headed for the bathroom.

Downstairs mum was making toast, Lewis avoided looking at the old-fashioned range cooker as he entered the scullery. Yet another scary thing to make him uneasy.

'I spoke to Mrs Featherstone, the lady with the puppies last night. She said we can go and see them today,' said mum.

She watched as Lewis firmly close the door between the scullery and the kitchen. He was clearly not comfortable with the features of the old house. Sadly, like many parents she thought that a distraction would work to make everything right. In this instance it seemed to work, Lewis's face lit up and he hurriedly ate his toast and headed for the front door.

'I'm ready when you are,' he said wiping crumbs from his chin.

'Not so fast, let's give them time to get up properly before we descend on them,' laughed mum, pleased to see a smile back on her son's face.

Mrs Featherstone had said come at eleven for coffee and cake, so Lewis decided to send the message and pictures to his pals before he forgot. Putting the whole episode of the mystery man and the strange sensation he had felt in the attic room out of his mind, Lewis focused on the promised puppy. A dog that he could train and play with would be fun! It was soon time to leave. Lewis stood by the car and wondered why mum was grinning.

'We're walking son, she just lives up the road next to the old orphanage. By the way what do you think about it being turned into a luxury hotel?' she asked.

Lewis had given the hotel little thought. If it improved the look of the building then he was all for it, but he wasn't going to say that to his mum. He was aware that she had been watching him all morning since he had come downstairs from the attic room. Perhaps she too had had the same sensation when she had been up there. But he would never know unless she told him, and he certainly had no intention of telling her what he had felt while in the attic room.

The walk to Mrs Featherstone's house took a matter of minutes. Mum was right to have suggested they walk, it was a beautiful warm summers day with not a cloud in the sky, Lewis imagined himself walking his new dog. The feeling felt good. As they passed the old orphanage Lewis stopped to take a closer look at the building. Until now he had only seen the place through his bedroom window, or in a picture. He wanted to take a closer look at it and try to get a feel for the type of place it once might have been. The large wrought iron gates were rusting, but still magnificent and impressive, they had to be almost 2 metres high.

'Was that to keep people out or the children in?' he muttered to himself.

He tried to imagine what it must have been like to be put into an orphanage because both your parents were dead. The images that filled his head were not pleasant, so he decided to save that thought for another day. However, curiosity got the better of him as he stood staring up at the tall dirty windows. What had the man been doing that morning? Apart from a curved line in the gravel where the gate had been pushed open there was no sign that anyone had been near the place for weeks or even months.

'Come on Lewis, what are you looking at?' he heard mum call over her shoulder. She had walked on and was now standing outside a picket fence. Hurrying to catch her up, Lewis once again tried to put the orphanage out of his mind.

Mrs Featherstone's house was set back from the road. It too was built of red brick and had the same long sash windows as The Old Rectory and the old orphanage.

'Why do all the buildings around here look alike?' asked Lewis.

'I believe they were all built together as part of the old Eden estate. That would be a nice project for you Lewis, to research the village and the Eden family.'

Lewis had already formed the same opinion but said nothing. At that moment the front door opened, and an enthusiastic golden cocker spaniel ran towards them. It was soon followed by another, both females but one clearly had recently given birth.

'Goldie! Honey! Get back here now,' came a deep booming voice followed by Mrs Featherstone. She was a large woman, tall and wide, some would have described her as 'big boned'. She had a kind red face and looked flustered as if she had too much to do and didn't know what to do first.

'Come in, come in, I was just getting some scones out of the oven, and then I thought the young man might not like scones so I decided to whip up some fairy cakes, I believe you young folk call them 'cup cakes', or even 'muffins', but in my day they were called fairy cakes. Get inside now before the dogs eat them all!'

And with that they were ushered into a swelteringly hot kitchen. Every conceivable surface was covered in baking implements, some Lewis and even mum had never seen before. Mrs Featherstone was clearly a keen cook and kept her tools of the trade close at hand.

'Sorry about the mess, but it's hard keeping on top of things with the dogs and puppies to look after,' she added by way of an apology. Lewis liked her instantly; her personality was as warm as her kitchen.

His eyes were drawn to a large pen in the corner of the kitchen in which were the most beautiful litter of pups Lewis had ever seen, not that he'd seen many! They were different shades of red, from a deep golden russet to a more apricot colour. All were scrambling to get out of the pen and play with their visitors. Mum was watching him again, but this time he could see she was smiling.

'What do you think Mr Woo?' she asked.

Now normally Lewis would have been cross with her for using his pet name in front of a stranger, but he somehow felt comfortable in the presence of Mrs Featherstone and didn't mind at all. The puppies were all he could think of, even the smell of the freshly baked cakes couldn't distract him away from the beautiful yelping bundles of fur.

'Your Mum said you wanted a girl or, to give them their correct name a bitch. I don't hold with all this namby pamby nonsense about using 'polite' words. Straight talking is my way. There's two bitches in the litter so you're a lucky young man as you get the first choice.'

Lewis smiled to himself, he knew mum would have something to say about Mrs Featherstonc's straight talking.

Mrs Featherstone picked up two of the puppies and held them out to Lewis.

'Sit down young man then you can have them on your lap. Best to see them both together so you can decide which one has taken to you and which one you've taken to.'

Lewis did as he was told and moving a pile of newspapers sat down in a much used wing backed chair. At that moment there was the sound of scratching and whining coming from the back door, Mrs Featherstone sighed and still holding the two puppies she managed to open the door with a wiggle of her hip and foot. Both Lewis and his mum turned instinctively towards the cool fresh air that wafted into the stiflingly hot kitchen. Two more dogs joined the now crowded room, one of the cocker spaniels he had seen earlier at the front door and a young apricot coloured cockapoo puppy. The puppy was older than the litter in the corner, but apart from that it was identical to the rest with the same rich apricot colouring. As Mrs Featherstone approached Lewis with the two new-born female pups, the older pup jumped up onto his lap.

'Well I never! She's normally so shy. Not even my granddaughter Lupin can get her to sit on her knee, that one likes you!'

The puppy set about giving Lewis's face a good wash, Lewis giggled as the puppy's tongue tickled his face. Leaning into Lewis, she snuggled into his T-shirt and swished her tail.

'Is this one for sale?' asked Lewis tentatively.

He liked the older woman and didn't want to offend her,

but something about the way the young puppy had gravitated towards him made him feel good. It was as if an instant bond had been formed between them.

Still holding the mewing pups Mrs Featherstone turned her head from Lewis to his mum and back to the pen of puppies. After a moment collecting her thoughts, she explained that the puppy Lewis was holding had been part of Goldie's litter six months earlier but being smaller and so shy they had not wanted to sell her. The new litter of puppies belonged to Honey, her other cocker spaniel, and these were the puppies that were for sale.

'Now, young man you've got me in a fix. I, or should I say we, thought we were keeping that little 'un. By the way we call her Bashful. Anyway, as I was saying she's a strange little creature and you're the first person she's taken to like that. We've tried all ways to make her feel loved, but she just follows her mum around and never wants a cuddle.'

Lewis's mum looked from her son to Mrs Featherstone, trying to follow the conversation. She looked totally confused. She had expected Lewis to be over the moon about the new-born puppies. They were adorable, tiny bundles of fluff, but here he was asking to have what was obviously the runt of another litter.

'What do you say Mum?' Mrs Featherstone asked, still holding the two pups.

'If it's okay with you its Lewis's choice,' mum said. Turning to Lewis she added. 'The dog is your responsibility. So, make a wise choice. There is no going back or changing your mind.'

'I'll have this one,' he said with confidence as he snuggled the puppy in his lap. 'I'm going to call her Truffle.'

'Well, well, that young man knows his own mind, I'm glad to see he's not a ditherer, I can't stand that in a person. Make your mind up is what I say. Well done lad! Now who wants some cake?'

Mrs Featherstone filled the kettle and hastily shifted some of the baking trays and clutter from one end of the table to the other, she set out cups and saucers and produced a delicate bone china tea pot.

'Tea or squash?' she asked as she reached for a large bottle of orange barley water and held it up to his mum. Lewis glared at his mum, wishing to make the point that he was a young adult and replied, 'Tea please.'

Mum's neck whipped round so quickly she surely must have jarred it!

'When did you start drinking tea?' she asked.

Lewis gave her a look that made it crystal clear he was not going to have this conversation now. It was a tactical move on his part. He also felt it might impress Mrs Featherstone. Much as he liked her, he was beginning to get a little annoyed that she seemed to speak to him through his mum. He wanted her to talk to him directly.

'I've heard drinking tea on a hot day is better at cooling you down,' he added in a knowledgeable voice.

Mum shook her head. If she carries on shaking her head like that she's going to cause herself some damage thought Lewis.

'You're absolutely right my man. What a clever boy you've got there, I think you'll like my granddaughter Lupin. Now there's a girl that knows what she likes and isn't afraid of saying so.' Mrs Featherstone chuckled as she thought of her granddaughter.

'How old are you? I've forgotten your name. Tell me again.'

Lewis couldn't help laughing. He could see his mum doing her best not to laugh too. She had picked up one of the puppies and now buried her face in its soft fur pretending she was smiling at something the pup had done.

'I'm Lewis,' said Lewis becoming very formal and holding out his hand to Mrs Featherstone for her to shake it.

'Forgive me Lewis, I've no manners. Lupin's always telling me off for talking too much. I can see you two getting on like a house on fire. But why it's called a house on fire I really don't know!'

Lewis was about to tell Mrs Featherstone that he was twelve but didn't get a chance. At that moment the back door was pushed further open and a lively poodle bounded into the room. The poodle was the same rich colouring as the puppy that Lewis had chosen; a beautiful shade of red, which some might have crudely called ginger.

'Here's dad, ain't he a pretty boy,' Mrs Featherstone said to no one in particular as she placed the bone china tea pot on the table and filled a plate with scones and fairy cakes. Jam, butter, milk and sugar were eventually brought to the table and they sat down to eat, but not before mum had suggested that she and Lewis both needed to visit the lavatory. Lewis had been waiting for this. Mum had to wash her hands before she could eat and insisted he did the same. She had even taken to putting hand gel in his school bag.

Mrs Featherstone looked puzzled but dutifully pointed them in the direction of the downstairs lavatory. Lewis waited outside while mum went in first and came out with damp hands. On his return to the kitchen Lewis could hear Mrs Featherstone on the telephone. It was possible that the whole village could hear her on the telephone. Her voice had gone up several notches and she sounded as if she were addressing royalty. Not wishing to listen in and not wanting to be rude Lewis walked towards the open back door and stepped out into the garden. Mum, who had been sitting awkwardly at the table, got up and joined him.

The garden was refreshingly cool after the heat of the kitchen. The sweet scent of roses drifted to their nostrils. Both the Featherstones must have been keen gardeners, as there was not a petal out of place or a weed to be seen. Lewis thought of his new garden at The Old Rectory and the sorry state it was in. It would take months to dig out the weeds alone. He knew who would most likely be assigned that job.

A voice was heard calling them back inside, Mrs Featherstone's hot face appeared as she suggested they return to the kitchen. She went on to tell them that the call had been from Addbridge Construction. The Featherstones were key holders for the old orphanage. She explained how a smart young man had asked if they minded having the keys to the building, as from time to time people would need access to it as they waited for the planning permission to be granted for the change of use. She added with a wide grin that they were even being paid for the privilege of holding a few keys.

After what seemed like an age Mrs Featherstone poured the now stewed tea, Lewis did his best to drink the disgusting drink and wondered how adults managed to force down so many cups of the stuff each day. The cakes however, were a different matter; they were heavenly, delicious and light. Lewis managed to eat two scones and one of the fairy cakes, before his mum told him that he had had enough. They left shortly afterwards. It had been agreed that Lewis would have Bashful, soon to be re-named Truffle, once they had got the necessary dog items. They agreed to collect her later that week.

The walk home was fun, mum seemed in a good mood. Mrs Featherstone had clearly lifted her spirits, which in turn made Lewis feel happier. When they reached the gates to the orphanage both stopped to take another look at the imposing building. As he looked up at the first floor Lewis was sure that he saw a face at one of the windows. He stared hard at the window but could see nothing, it must have been his imagination. Mrs Featherstone had told them the place was empty - and the keys had been pointed to on the dresser.

Chapter 5

The Breakout 1860

As The Master sipped his whisky, he listened for the sound of an owl hooting. This was his signal that the job had been successfully completed, and the boys were back. A window in the scullery would be left open to allow the boys to sneak back into the orphanage. Once back inside, The Master would hurry them into the dining room cum work room where they would sleep until morning. This gave the impression that they had been hard at work all night as a punishment. If Tom or any other member of staff happened to see The Master in the corridor with a boy, he would make a great pretence of scolding the boy before pushing him into the dining room. On these occasions Mike Unwin made it patently clear to the staff that no one apart from himself was to enter the dining room. The staff not wishing to have any extra duties thrust upon them, were happy to leave him to supervise the night work force.

There it was – the signal. He hastily swallowed the whisky and headed for the door. At that moment the upper floor was filled with the sound of splintering wood, running feet and uproar. Something was up! And he needed to get to the bottom of it quickly. If the robbery had gone to plan four fat pouches would have been dropped outside the study window and the boys would be waiting in the scullery. What on earth had gone wrong?

He rushed from the study. Intoxicated by the whisky, Mike Unwin had little time to assess the situation. Puffing and panting from running up the stairs he surveyed the scene. On the landing several of the male and female staff were gathered at the door of the male dormitory. Tom was rubbing his head and shouting at the boys to get back into bed. They were having none of it! This was far too much fun! A crowd had clustered around the door to gape at the broken lock.

'They've gone, they've gone,' cried Tom to the other staff members. Counting wasn't one of his talents, but a hasty scan of the faces around the door told him that at least four of the boys were missing.

'This is bad!' The Master exclaimed to no one in particular.

'Out of my way,' he added as he rushed into the dormitory looking from face to face in an attempt to spot who was missing.

'Get back into bed at once,' he bellowed.

This worked and the boys suddenly became quiet and hastily did as they were told. Something wasn't right. Only four beds should have been empty, but he counted eight. Also, as his brain began to process the situation he realised that the broken lock was unusual. His boys would have no need to break into the dormitory, and why were there so many empty beds?

'Why are these beds empty?' he screamed at the frightened Tom. 'You secured the door as always didn't you?'

As his mind became clearer, he was beginning to feel somewhat uneasy, he wasn't sure if the sensation in his stomach was due to the whisky or the situation in front of him. The staff were whispering and nudging one another. He was aware that although not usually a bright bunch, they were drawing their own conclusions as to what had taken place that night. Village gossip had been circulating suggesting that perhaps some of the local robberies had been the work of the children from the orphanage. The Master had always been keen to scotch such rumours, and had even invited the newly formed police force to search both the male and female dormitories secure in the knowledge that they would find nothing.

By now all the inhabitants of the orphanage were awake, they had never had so much fun! The children and staff looked on as The Master's face changed from its usual putty grey complexion to a bright crimson. With each breath he became more heated and irate. Why did he care so much about a few parentless boys? His anger seemed a little too excessive.

Gradually and with a great deal of shouting, order was restored. All the children were once more back in their beds and the staff were assembled in their common room. Tom had been told he was to sleep on the landing outside the male dormitory, partly as punishment for allowing the boys to break out in the first place and also as a deterrent to others who might think that they could do the same. The Master was becoming more agitated by the minute. He knew that the loot had been dropped outside the study window and no doubt his lads were anxiously waiting in the scullery for him to escort them to the work room. It would have been impossible for them not to have heard the earlier commotion.

'Hold your nerve Mike,' he told himself.

All eyes were on him as he addressed the assembled staff.

'They won't get far, and we'll pick them up in the morning,' he announced with confidence. 'Go to bed now, and I'll do my rounds to make sure the building is secure,' he added.

He was keen to be alone. He still had the problem of the lads in the scullery who could be discovered at any moment by an interfering member of staff, but being a greedy and self-centred man he decided he had better collect up the pouches first before going to the scullery. The welfare of the loot was of far more importance than his four young thieves. Opening the front door, he turned left in the direction of Joshua Eden's open study window. Several of the plants in the border showed signs of having been trodden on, but this was of little consequence to him. His eyes now accustomed to the dark, Mike Unwin knelt down to search for the cotton pouches that the boys customarily used to stow the stolen jewels. He soon found what he was looking for and picked up three weighty pouches. On any other such occasion he would have been grinning from ear to ear, in anticipation of the contents of each pouch. This evening he was eager to simply gather up the loot and stow it safely away until the morning.

'One more Mike,' he told himself, then he would decide what to do with the idiots who thought they could run away from his care. But search as he might, the ground yielded up nothing apart from soil, stones and plants. Nothing out of the ordinary was to be found under the bush or in the nearby border.

'The thieving swines,' he exclaimed as his brain told him that the missing pouch had to have been taken by someone else, and that someone else had to be one of the idiot boys who thought that they could run away from the orphanage. One of the boys must have found it as they jumped from the window. This was serious, he mused, if he didn't retrieve it soon, the stolen items would lead straight back to the orphanage and all his years of hard work would be undone! He decided that the best course of action was to deal with one problem at a time. His head was now thumping from all the excitement and the whisky.

Making his way to the scullery, he found his little band of thieves wide awake.

The Breakout 1860

'What's up?' asked one of the boys.

'It's all sweet aint it?' asked another now visibly worried.

'Nowt to worry about,' replied The Master. 'Just some idiots think they can leave this place,' he added, trying to make light of the situation but feeling anything but confident.

Fortunately for Mike Unwin the boys accepted his explanation and, tired from their night time antics, they dutifully followed him into the workroom and settled down to sleep. Sleep was furthermost from The Master's mind. Before the return of Joshua Eden, he had to retrieve the lost pouch, silence the boys who had stolen it and have all of them back in the orphanage working away as if nothing had happened. Added to this was the knowledge that morning would bring an enthusiastic police officer, once the robbery was discovered. All had to appear normal to avoid suspicion. He knew the staff were watching him, he had heard some of the village gossip which suggested that the inhabitants of the orphanage were in some way involved in the spate of local burglaries. Someone on the staff might talk to the police and they in turn might decide to keep a closer eye on the orphanage. He decided that he was going to have to lie low for a while and let things blow over. The three pouches were safely hidden.

Ned, Robert, Herbert and George had made it to a disused barn, on the far field of Joshua Eden's land. No-one had used the barn for years, and the field had been left unplanted. They had planned to separate and take their chances alone. They knew that The Master and staff would be searching for them as a group, and to be seen together would arouse suspicion. That fateful June night they could never have guessed that they would be hunted down as criminals who had stolen from the hand that fed them. On reaching the barn all were both exhausted and excited.

They had got away from the clutches of The Master and his cane touting staff. Throwing themselves onto a pile of hay they all talked at once about their daring deed.

'What's up George?' asked Ned, noticing that George had become strangely quiet.

In place of words George pulled the cotton pouch from his pocket and tipped its contents onto the dirty barn floor. The atmosphere in the barn suddenly became charged with nervous energy. In the dim moonlight, all were quiet as they gazed at the beautiful glittering diamond and ruby pendant and its matching earrings. They had all seen them before, not like this, but rather on the person of Mrs Eden. Why then and how had George got hold of them?

'I jumped on it, honest,' said George, by way of an explanation. Ned, Herbert and Robert were now squinting hard at him.

George explained how he had twisted his ankle and when he had bent down to see what had caused it, had found the pouch. Not having time to look inside he had simply stuffed it in his pocket and ran. Once they had put some distance between themselves and the orphanage, he had pulled the pouch from his pocket and taken a quick look inside. He was as perplexed as the others. How, why and when had Mrs Eden's jewels been left outside an open window?

'We can't keep 'em, we'll be hung,' wailed Robert.

'No one will believe we just found 'em either,' added Ned. The three boys looked at George as if expecting some words of wisdom.

'I didn't nick owt, yous were with me the whole time, and anyway where did I nick em from? I've never been to Eden's house,' George pleaded loudly.

The boys knew in that instant that their little plan of escaping for a better life had gone horribly wrong. The Edens would want their property returned, but how to do that and still escape the noose? No one would believe they had simply found the jewellery on the ground. The boys, of course, knew nothing of the robbery at the home of the Eden family. However, each knew enough of life to know that Mrs Eden would not have put her beautiful jewels in a tatty cotton pouch. Neither would she have been careless enough to drop the said pouch in the grounds of the orphanage.

Chapter 6

A new Friend 2019

Plans for the arrival of the puppy were racing around in Lewis's head. Like his mother Lewis loved to write a list and tick things off as they had been completed. His list for the puppy had now spread onto two pages. Mum had laughed properly for the first time in ages when she'd seen the list, which had brought tears to Lewis's eyes. At the tender age of 12 he suddenly realised how unhappy his mum must have been for the past few years. He tried to remember when he had last seen her this happy and couldn't ever remember her looking so relaxed.

'Why are you laughing Mum?' he had asked as he turned away so that she would not see the tears in his eyes.

'I'm trying to work out where we are going to put all the stuff you're asking for, and how I will be able to pay for it all,' she answered.

'A puppy will need a bed, food and water and that's it! Oh! And yes, most importantly she will need love,' mum explained.

'There'll be no shortage of love that's for sure,' said Lewis, picking up his lists and screwing up his face as he looked for items to strike off. There did seem to be rather a lot of toys. Perhaps mum was right, Truffle would be happy being cuddled and running around at his side.

Lewis sat at the kitchen table deep in thought about his new friend Truffle. He decided to send a text message and photo of the puppy to his old friends. Getting out his phone he realised it had not been charged for some time, so he went upstairs in search of the charger. Mum had now turned her attention to yet more unpacking, and was actually humming, something Lewis had never heard her do before.

On the landing outside his bedroom door, Lewis glanced at the attic stairs. A thin shaft of light could be seen shining onto the bare pine floorboards. What was it about that attic room that left him feeling so uncomfortable? Turning, he tried to dismiss the feeling of sadness that had come over him as he looked at the stairs.

'It's all in your imagination,' Lewis whispered to himself.

Purposefully he turned and stepped into his bedroom. It took him some time to find the phone charger, as his room was still a sea of boxes. Plugging in the phone Lewis turned to the window and stood contemplating the beauty of the open countryside. There was not a sound apart from that of the sheep in the field and birdsong. His eyes were drawn to a lone rider, cycling down the lane from the direction of Mrs Featherstone's house towards Church Lane and The Old Rectory.

As the figure came into view Lewis saw that it was a girl of a similar age to himself. As if sensing that she was being watched she turned her head and looked directly at Lewis. The action in itself took a matter of seconds but, rather than feeling foolish and wanting to duck away from the window Lewis found himself waving at the girl as if she were a long-lost friend. The girl lifted her left arm to indicate that she was turning left into Church Lane and smiled at Lewis. Phone and charger forgotten; Lewis raced from his bedroom downstairs to the front door. For some reason he felt a need to speak to the girl; she was the first young person he had seen since the move to Nottinghamshire a few days earlier. In London he had a whole string of friends whom he saw almost daily. Much as he was enjoying spending time with his mum, he missed the company of other young people. As luck would have it, the girl had stopped in the lane outside his new home.

Throwing open the front door Lewis suddenly felt stupid. Why was he racing after this complete stranger? She probably thought he was some sort of fruit cake waving at her when he didn't even know her. Stopping in the doorway Lewis pretended to be calling his dog.

'Truffle where are you girl? Good girl,' he shouted in a strange high pitched and extremely false voice. He stepped outside and pretended to be looking for the imaginary dog.

'If you're looking for Truffle she's at me Gran's,' laughed the girl, as she leant her bike against the rectory wall. 'It's a nice name and it suits her, but I doubt if she can hear you from here.'

Her face was flushed from the bike ride, her long blonde hair tied up into a neat ponytail. She was pulling something from her jeans pocket. Seeing what was in her hand Lewis blushed deeply and wished he had never opened the front door.

'Gran said you left this behind in the toilet,' said the girl grinning now at Lewis's obvious discomfort. She held out the small plastic bottle of hand sanitizer.

'Oh, that will be my Mum's,' Lewis replied trying to pass off his discomfort. 'She's obsessed with germs,' he laughed.

'Whatever. I'm Lupin by the way, and I take it you must be Lewis?'

'That's me. Give me that and I'll make sure Mum gets it,' Lewis said as he reached out to take the bottle of hand sanitizer from the girl called Lupin.

Lupin held the bottle out to Lewis and deliberately held onto it as he made to take it from her hand. Lewis felt such a fool. He couldn't understand why such a normal item should cause him so much embarrassment. But something about Lupin's confident nature had made him feel a bit of a sissy.

To change the subject Lewis asked Lupin if she would like a glass of water and to meet his mum. The two young people stepped into the house and headed for the kitchen, where his mum was now singing at full volume, and it was not a pleasant sound!

'She'll think we're mad,' thought Lewis. 'I'll never have any friends at this rate, and I bet she'll tell everyone at school so I'm a laughingstock before I've even started there in September!'

Seeing Lewis and Lupin entering the kitchen mum had the good grace to stop singing and step forward to welcome their first visitor.

'Hello, and who might you be?' she asked stretching out her hand to Lupin.

'I'm Lupin, me Gran's Mrs Featherstone, and she said your son left some hand stuff behind in her downstairs bog and I was to bring it round straight away in case he needed it urgent.' Suppressing a laugh she went on to say, 'she thought he might have some sort of illness that means he's got to keep his hands extra clean.'

Lewis was fuming. It was clear Lupin was enjoying his embarrassment and wasn't prepared to leave the subject alone. Mum, picking up on her son's discomfort, took the small bottle and placed it in her handbag which lay on the kitchen table.

'Thank you, Lupin, I never go anywhere without it.' And with that, that conversation was closed.

'Can I offer you some refreshment?' Mum asked, opening the fridge. 'Lewis, I'm sure there's a packet of biscuits in the pantry. Get them out please and offer one to Lupin.'

Glad of a chance to compose himself, Lewis opened the pantry and stepping over even more boxes, found a packet of chocolate biscuits. The kitchen was a mess, wrapping paper strewn across the floor and items of crockery and cutlery on every surface. Lewis could see Lupin looking around the room and taking in every detail. This was not a good start, but then again she did know that they had only just moved in a few days ago.

Clearing a space on the dresser Lewis emptied the packet of biscuits onto the plate. He found two tumblers and held up a bottle of orange squash. Lupin nodded and sat at the table. Having mixed the squash Lewis also sat down. Mum excused herself and went into the scullery to continue unpacking even more boxes onto the floor.

'Sorry about earlier. I didn't mean to be cruel I was just having fun,' said Lupin smiling as she helped herself to a chocolate biscuit. 'These are good. Would you believe we never have shop bought biscuits in my house? Me Gran makes all her own biscuits, cakes and jams and Mum's the same.'

'My Mum used to bake a lot but my dad preferred the shop stuff so she gave up,' Lewis found himself confessing.

He felt sad at the mention of his father. He hadn't spoken to him that day and was not looking forward to the evening phone call when dad would quiz him about his new home and what they had been up to. He felt as if he were being torn in two. On the one hand he wanted to be loyal to his mum and she didn't want dad knowing too much about their new lives, while on the other hand he could hear the pain in dad's voice at losing his son.

'I'm hoping Mum might start baking again now we're in the country, isn't it what all country folk do?' he added.

The two children both reached for another biscuit and Lewis

put the whole biscuit in his mouth and scoffed it loudly. It broke the ice, and Lupin not wishing to be left out did the same.

'So, you're having Bashful? I like the name you've chosen for her, Truffle is much nicer. Me Granddad hasn't much imagination when it comes to naming dogs, but then again he's had to make up names for loads of dogs over the years.'

And that's how the friendship started. Lupin filled Lewis in on the village and who was who. They discovered they were the same age with only weeks between them and would be attending the same secondary school in September. Lupin was also an only child and was used to spending most of her summer holidays with her grandparents, as both her parents worked full time in the city of Nottingham. Lewis explained that his mum was a teacher but had given up her job and would be looking for supply work in the autumn term. It was clear that Lupin knew that his parents had separated, but she never mentioned it, or asked Lewis about his dad. She had seen the hurt in his eyes when he had alluded to his dad's preference for shop bought biscuits. After what seemed a matter of minutes Lupin got up to leave saying that her gran would have her lunch ready and be wondering where she had got to. They agreed to meet the next day. Lewis was invited to lunch at Mrs Featherstone's and after much pleading with his mum he had persuaded her that it was perfectly safe for him to take his bike up to the Featherstones' house. Lupin had suggested that after lunch she could give him a tour of the village, which had delighted Lewis.

The rest of the day passed without event for Lewis. He helped his mum unpack and find homes for their various personal items and organise the kitchen into a tidier more manageable space. By evening both were tired and dusty and in need of a hot bath. As they climbed the stairs to their bedrooms, Lewis asked his mum what she thought of the attic rooms.

'They're a bit dirty and tired but I'm sure we can make them more inviting.'

'No, I don't mean that! Don't they make you feel all goose bumpy?'

'Goose bumpy? Why? They're just in need of TLC. Don't go imagining things Lewis!'

With that she headed for the bathroom and began to run a bath. But that wasn't the end of that conversation for Lewis. Something about the two rooms, in particular the larger of the two overlooking the garden, made him feel uneasy. Perhaps it was a ghost, after all, the house was over 100 years old, and people did die in houses! Taking a deep breath Lewis decided to go up to the creepy room and take some photos. He collected his now charged mobile phone, quickly sent a text and photo of Truffle to Alfie and informed him of his new friend Lupin. Feeling bolder he headed up the steep stairs.

The landing light bulb must have been the lowest wattage possible. It barely threw any light on the staircase and landing. Opening the door to the larger of the bedrooms, Lewis felt an icy draft as if a window had suddenly been opened on a frosty day, but the window was shut.

'It's in your head Lewis,' he said aloud.

The floorboards creaked, some even moved as he stepped over them. Dad would have got his tool kit out and nailed them down straight away, but he doubted that mum would even notice. Her plans for the house didn't seem to include the attic rooms. The rusting cast iron fireplace had a smattering of soot in the grate covering the bird droppings. Lewis knew that the soot had not been there before. Thinking rationally, he reasoned that it must have blown down the chimney since his previous visit. But even that explanation didn't satisfy him, there had been no wind, in fact this was one of the hottest and driest summers on record according the BBC News. So, where had the soot come from?

Thinking no more of this, Lewis heard his mum calling up the stairs, telling him to hang up his clothes and tidy his room. Mum had now unpacked all of his clothes and had pointedly laid them on his bed. For almost two weeks, Lewis had ignored the growing pile of clothes, and had simply swept them onto the floor each night. If he was to sleep in the bed that night, he would have to move them and soon. There was little enough space on the floor to move around the overcrowded room, let alone add to the mess with a further pile of clothes. Lewis knew that mum had turned a blind eye to the mess in his room, aware of his uncertainty about the divorce and move. But enough was enough, he felt the time had come to show her that he could be sensible and helpful. He would make a start now and put away his clothes. On the right-hand side of the fireplace stood a large oak wardrobe. It must have been built into the room, as there was no way that it could have fitted through the door or even the window. Sighing, Lewis opened the double doors. Mum had cleaned it out, there was none of the customary cobwebs that seemed to linger in every corner of the house.

Inside was a full width hanging rail, with a recessed shelf above it. The base of the wardrobe was some twenty centimetres off the floor. As he stood looking up at the large floor to ceiling storage space, he wondered how he was to reach the ridiculously high-top shelf. Picking up a pile of jumpers and hoodies he considered the best approach. The simplest solution seemed to be to stand just inside the doors, on the base of the wardrobe, and somehow throw the tops onto the shelf. After all it was summer, and he wouldn't be needing them for some time. He could have a proper sort out at the end of summer.

Cautiously he stepped into the wardrobe, the base felt solid enough to take his weight.

'Proper carpentry,' muttered Lewis in imitation of his father.

Stepping down from the wardrobe Lewis picked up a pile of hoodies and holding them in one hand he stepped back into the wardrobe. He held the clothes rail with his left hand as he leant back, intending to throw the clothes up onto the shelf. There was a loud crack and Lewis felt himself slipping backwards. His grip on the clothes rail loosened as the baseboard tipped him out of the wardrobe and onto the floor.

'Blimey! that was close,' he exclaimed to the empty room, when he realised that another few centimetres further back and he would have hit his head on the bedpost.

The wardrobe baseboard was now sticking up at a strange angle, rather like a fat sea saw. Getting up and catching his breath, Lewis stepped over to the wardrobe intent on pushing the baseboard back down and having another go at throwing his hoodies onto the top shelf. As he tried to line up the board, something caught his eye in the space below. It was the corner of what looked like an old newspaper. It was carefully folded and looked as though it had been deliberately placed in the cavity.

The newspaper was clearly very old and faded. Lewis could barely make out a date, September 1860. Over 150 years before he had been born! Perhaps it was valuable. He tried to unfold it and read what was in the news in the 1860's. Finding a carrier bag he carefully placed the newspaper in the bag. He then opened his chest of drawers and placed the newspaper in the bottom drawer. He decided that an internet search might be in order to find out what was in the news in September 1860. Something about the way in which he had found the newspaper made him feel that this was not a topic to share with his already stressed mother. He felt certain that someone had carefully placed or hidden the newspaper under the baseboard in the wardrobe for a reason. It must have lain hidden for over 150 years. But what was its significance?

Mum's head appeared round his bedroom door to tell him that she had finished in the bathroom and had run him a bath. After a long soak and good scrub, Lewis finally fired up his laptop. His mother had gone to bed, so he knew that if he was quiet she would not be aware that he was still awake. There were plenty of messages from his old school friends and lots of silly photos from the football team he had played for. It took several attempts to find what he was looking for. The old newspaper was *The Nottingham Journal*, which had carried a sensational story of a court case, in which a James Cooper age 14, had been found guilty of burglary and theft in 1860.

Chapter 7

The Master's Fury 1860

After a disturbed night's sleep, Mike Unwin woke to yet another bright and sunny day. He had overslept and his head still ached from the whisky. Hurrying to wash and dress he rushed to the work room. His four accomplices were fast asleep on the benches and floor. One had even found a sack of flour to use as a pillow. There was no time for niceties, the boys needed to be moved before the staff woke and began to prepare the breakfast of a watery porridge.

'Wake up, and look alive, we've no time for slacking,' he called to the sleeping boys, as he glanced out of the window to hastily check that there was no one in the back yard. The boys were ushered outside, and each handed a broom.

'Sweep,' he told them, and they did.

There were soon noises from inside the building which told him that the staff and children were awake. A female house mistress popped her head around the back door with a look of surprise on her face.

'You've got them working hard, what they have done to deserve this?' she asked.

The common practice was that after a 'night of work' the boys would usually be allowed to return to the dormitory for a few hours' sleep. Mike never questioned how long they slept for, as this was part of their reward for a successful robbery. While some of the staff might have queried this method of punishment, none dared to voice their thoughts to The Master himself.

'How did last night go?' he whispered as he walked close to the group of boys.

He was conscious that with the orphanage awake he might be watched by the children and staff who had marvelled at the drama of the previous evening.

'I'm a bag down,' he added. 'Any idea what happened to it?'

The boys continued to sweep the yard. One walked over to a water trough as if to fetch water. The Master followed. At a distance from the building they were able to talk without the chance of anyone overhearing them.

'We got some real beauties,' said the boy whose name was Charlie. 'Even that fancy stuff that Her Ladyship wears on Sundays in church, them big rubies and the matching earrings, bet they're worth a bob or two,' he added with a grin of satisfaction.

The 'fancy stuff' he had referred to was a particularly ostentatious diamond and ruby pendant with matching earrings. The rubies were almost the size of wrens eggs and the diamonds the size of peppercorns. Many a child and indeed adult had marvelled at the strength of her ladyship's neck in its ability to carry the weight of the jewels!

Mike was confused, before going to bed he had taken a quick look in the three pouches and had felt his customary warm glow of satisfaction creep over his thin body. He knew that there was still one pouch to be retrieved along with the idiot boys who had dared to attempt to escape his care. What he hadn't known up until now was what was in the missing pouch.

Mrs Eden's ruby and diamond pendant with the matching earrings had been the talk of the village when her husband had presented them to her on the birth of their twin daughters. All who saw them had marvelled at his generosity, they were truly a statement piece that told of the man's immense wealth and his love for his wife. This could only mean one thing, the 'lost' pouch contained the ruby and diamond pendant and their matching earrings, amongst other items he had yet to feast his eyes on. Thinking quickly, he knew he had to try to restore order within the orphanage and find out who had broken out. The runaways needed to be found, and soon, by him and no one else. No policeman or well-meaning nosy parker must find the boys first, particularly if they still had 'his' goods upon their person. Punishment for their folly would be dished out later, once he had all the stolen items in his possession.

Leaving the boys to continue with sweeping the yard he headed for the male dormitory. Tom and another member of staff were supervising the boys as they washed and readied themselves for another day in the blistering heat working in the fields or the gardens of the Manor house.

'Who's missing?' he asked of no one in particular.

Tom reeled off the names of the eight boys. The Master appeared not to be listening. You could almost see the cogs turning in his cunning brain as he tried to come up with a plan. He listened intently for the names of the missing boys, George, Ned, Robert and Herbert. How had these docile and until now hard-working idiots got the better of him? Tom watched in disbelief as The Master's face became infused with blood and his jaw began to work at grinding his teeth. Without another word he stormed down the stairs and out of the front door.

He needed air; he was struggling to breathe. His heart was trying to punch its way out of his chest.

'This is bad, bad and bad,' he muttered to himself as he walked in the direction of the study window.

Looking around to make sure no one was watching, but also feeling so desperate that he couldn't have cared if he had been watched, he searched once again under the bush just in case he had missed the pouch in the dark. Nothing but dirt. The ground was dry and contained the expected plants, stones and a few weeds. He even shook the rhododendron bush, just in case one of the dopey boys had flung the bag into the foliage.

As he stood in contemplation, he tried to piece together the events of the previous evening. Firstly, he needed a plan to retrieve the jewellery pouch without casting suspicion on himself. Considering each of the runaway boys in turn he realised he knew little if anything at all about the group apart from George. Until now the only one of the four that he had spoken to or, to be more truthful, shouted at had been George. He had on many an occasion had to abuse the boy for being too slow and sickly.

'The halfwit,' he shouted, then looked around guiltily in case someone had heard him.

Fortunately he was alone, the staff and children were inside no doubt eating their breakfast and preparing for the day ahead. 'The Halfwit' (as he had called George), was close to the Cooper boy, James. He would question James and find out what he knew about the breakout and if he knew where the boys might be hiding. He knew that James was protective of his sister, and he decided if it became necessary, he would use his power to threaten to have Millie dismissed in disgrace from The Rectory and sent to The Workhouse. The boy was bound to tell him what he knew if he thought that withholding information would lead to him losing his precious sister. As the cogs turned in his devious and evil brain, he decided that the best approach might be to befriend Cooper, if at all possible. Once he had extracted the information on the whereabouts of the little gang, he would throw him and the others to the authorities, but not before he had retrieved the pendant and earrings and whatever other gems might be in the missing pouch. After all who would care about a poor orphan boy? He would be just one less mouth to feed.

Chapter 8

Lewis Dreams of Millie 2019

That night Lewis found himself dreaming of the house that he now called home. In his dream the Rectory was back to its Victorian splendour. His own bedroom had a roaring fire burning in the grate and heavy drapes at the window. His dreams flitted from the past to the present. Someone called Millie was calling him and tell him to search, but search for what?

Who was Millie? He had a vague impression of a tall slim girl, with curly brown hair, not much older than himself. The girl wore a worried expression on her face. Her clothes were similar to those that Mrs Drew had borrowed from the museum for their Victorian topic at school. Not the elegant flowing dresses that the rich had worn, but rougher and plainer, she must have been a servant of some sort. The voice was more insistent now.

'Search please, help me!'

'Help us, please!'

'Lewis, darling whatever is the matter? You must have been having a nightmare.' Mum was sitting on his bed stroking his head.

It took several seconds for Lewis to shake off the impression that there was more than just the two of them in the room. Was he imagining it or had a figure quietly slipped out of the room as his mum reached for the bedside lamp?

'I'm okay Mum, just a bad dream. Go back to bed, I'll be fine.'

Lewis wanted his mum to go. Too much was going on in his head and in his room. He could have sworn the girl had stepped back into the room and was now standing behind the open door, but was she real or was he still dreaming? Mum got up from the bed and walked over to the door. Sitting up in bed Lewis stared hard at the door as mum closed it. There was nobody there. It must have been his imagination. He got out of bed and logged onto his computer. The internet search containing the archived newspaper story. Who was James Cooper? He reached for the printer and took out a sheet of paper. On it he wrote the following:

Find out:
Who was James Cooper?
Where did he live?
Did he have any family?
Is he linked to this house?
What did he steal?
Who is Millie?

Turning off the light Lewis lay awake for some time. He could not shake the feeling that he was not alone. Twice he reached for the bedside light and turned it on and off in quick succession hoping to catch whoever it was that was lurking in his room. Each time the room was empty apart from himself and the piles of clothes on the floor. He eventually fell into a deep sleep and slept soundly until the morning when he woke uttering 'Millie'.

Mum was once again wearing her worried face. She hovered

around Lewis as he ate his breakfast, and even suggested that as he had had a bad night it might be an idea to cancel lunch at Mrs Featherstone's. Lewis was adamant that he was fine and was looking forward to riding his bike again. Realising she was not going to win this argument, his mum gave in and continued with her never ending task of unpacking. The puzzle for Lewis was where was she going to put it all? Most of the unpacked items were simply sitting on the floor beside the boxes. Lewis spent the morning checking his bike, not that he knew what he was doing, but he felt the need to be out of the house.

The removal men had left his bike in what passed for a garage. It was nothing more than an old shed. Lewis sat on the patio looking down the garden. He could not shake off the feeling that he was being watched. Going back into the house through the former scullery which mum had now taken to calling the utility room, Lewis found himself reaching for the keys to the coal house and outside toilet. Turning the key in the lock of the coal house door Lewis stepped into the dark and dust filled room. He remembered that there was a light switch on one of the walls, so he ran his hand along the wall till he found it. The light bulb threw little light on the small blackened room. The central heating boiler stood silent in one corner, and apart from the dirt and cobwebs the room held nothing more. As he turned to leave Lewis caught a fleeting glimpse of a long off-white skirt as if someone had run from the room. Rushing outside into the garden he searched the immediate area for the person who had just left the room but could see no one. Was he going mad? Maybe this is what divorce did to kids! Had parents thought about how a divorce and upheaval might affect a young person?

Putting the keys back on their hook, Lewis spent the rest of the morning helping mum to unpack even more of the boxes in his bedroom. His friends (or toys as mum called them) were now arranged on shelves either side of the fireplace. Even though he had long since grown out of playing with soft toys he liked to keep them close as a reminder of happier times. It was finally 12:45, Lupin had said come for lunch at 1pm. Lewis knew it would take a matter of minutes to reach her grandparents' house, but he was eager to escape the endless task of unpacking, and more importantly he wanted to ask her and her grandparents what they knew about The Old Rectory.

Turning right at the end of Church Lane Lewis estimated it would take five minutes to reach the Featherstones' house by bike. Setting the stopwatch on his phone, Lewis began to cycle up the slight incline towards the Featherstones' house. The journey took all of three minutes. He was early, so he decided that he might as well take a look at the old orphanage. The gates were padlocked, and the place appeared to be totally deserted. White van man had probably been nothing more than someone lost or just taking a look at the old building. After all it certainly was impressive and intimidating at the same time. He could see how with imagination and money it could be turned into a beautiful country hotel.

At Mrs Featherstone's Lewis was introduced to Lupin's granddad, who had been out fishing the previous day. The old man proudly told Lewis that he was 86, and still going strong. The puppies were yelping, and Lewis was overcome with joy at the reception he received from Bashful, newly renamed Truffle. Mrs Featherstone asked what time he and his mum would be collecting Truffle later that week. Lewis realised that his mum had forgotten to sort this out and said he would speak to her that evening.

The lunch was delicious. When Lewis had been a small boy he used to make a fuss about eating 'flowers,' which had been his name for salad. Today, however, the salad was perfect, home grown crisp crunchy vegetables served with ham and a melt in the mouth quiche. Lewis had always thought his mum was a good cook, but Mrs Featherstone took cooking to a new level. Every morsel of food was eaten from his plate and more! The choice of desserts was amazing, so he had to try at least two. Lupin laughed as she watched him gorge his way through the meal.

'Mum's been too busy to cook since we moved,' he explained.

'Not a problem young man, I like to see you youngsters enjoy your food,' chuckled Mrs Featherstone.

After lunch Lewis and Lupin went into the garden to play with the dogs. Not wanting to waste a minute, Lewis quickly blurted out the events of the previous evening. He described the image of a girl fleetingly leaving the coal house. He had expected Lupin to laugh and mock him for mentioning a ghost, instead she became very quiet and suggested that Lewis told his tale to her grandparents. Mr and Mrs Featherstone sat perfectly still, as if watching a school play as they listened to what Lewis had to say. The story of James Cooper was known to all in the village, it was just a matter of time before Lewis and his mum would be told the tale of the boy who stole from the hand that fed him. James Cooper was a bad lot and his sister Millie had had to live with the shame of his crime for the rest of her short life.

'Me gran used to say she didn't understand why the Reverend and his wife didn't throw the girl out, but they kept her on just the same and she even died there in your house,' Mrs Featherstone explained. 'I hope you're not afraid of ghosts Lewis? Because some say she's still in the house!'

'Don't be frightening the young lad Jilly,' said Mr Featherstone seeing the look of horror that had now settled on Lewis's face.

Mr Featherstone went on to explain that James and Millie

Cooper had been orphans and had both lived in the old orphanage. Millie had been taken in by the then Reverend, Archibald Peabody and his wife Cynthia as a servant. When James was found guilty of robbing the home of the great Joshua Eden the whole of Kingminster had wanted to see him hang.

'Some say Joshua Eden didn't believe the boy was guilty, but he was found guilty by the Judge, and was never seen again,' added Mrs Featherstone.

Both went on to explain how Millie had remained in the village and had died at The Rectory.

'None of the stuff he stole was ever found, apart from one signet ring, so the story goes,' Mrs Featherstone continued. 'At Christmas the Eden family usually invite all the village up to the Manor House for drinks. You and your mum will get an invite. When you're there take a look at the portrait of his great-grandfather and great-grandmother. She's wearing the most magnificent necklace and matching earrings I've ever seen. They were part of the stuff stolen way back in 1860, and James Cooper never said what he did with them.'

'I'm still not sure the lad was actually guilty, after all he was only 14 at the time and he was accounted for on the night of the robbery,' added Mr Featherstone.

The story of James Cooper and his sister Millie was most definitely one that Lewis was keen to research. Forget the ugly orphanage and the houses in the village, he was now champing at the bit to get onto his laptop. Who would have guessed that Kingminster would be such a colourful place!

Mr Featherstone went on to add, 'There's been some strange happenings in this village over the years, all to do with the Rectory and the Orphanage. Things had settled down for years, but now the Orphanage is sold it seems to have stirred things up again.'

Chapter 9

Who's To Blame ? 1860

Millie was enjoying her life at The Rectory, Cynthia had agreed that her education should continue, and to this end Millie would accompany her to the orphanage on the days she taught there. This was a dream for Millie, who wasn't boastful or proud, but couldn't help feeling extremely happy at how her life had improved. On the Tuesday morning Millie knew the moment she walked into the orphanage that something was wrong. The atmosphere was different. It had never been a happy place, but today an air of despondency mingled with fear hung like a black cloud over all the inhabitants that she encountered. There was little chance to talk to any of the girls before the lesson began, but she knew that something serious had happened. Cynthia too was distracted. After the class she quickly dismissed the girls and told Millie to go home immediately. This in itself was unusual. Until now Millie had been allowed to linger at the orphanage and meet with James before she had to return to her duties at the Rectory. Once Cynthia was out of sight Millie grabbed the arm of the nearest girl.

'What's up? Something's wrong,' she asked.

The girl, not wishing to be seen and worrying for her safety, pulled Millie back into the school room quietly closing the door and leaning her back against it. She hurriedly told Millie what she knew of the night's events. On hearing George's name Millie instantly thought of James. She knew he would be worried for his young friend. She also knew that George was not one of life's survivors. He had arrived at the orphanage on the same day as herself and James, and a bond of friendship had formed between the three children. Millie had seldom seen George up close for some time, as the girls were kept separate from the boys. George was a sickly child and in constant need of medical attention, but that didn't mean he received any. Millie knew she had to speak to James and find out what if anything he knew of where the boys might be hiding. As the two girls left the school room, Millie was just in time to see The Master escorting two police officers into Mr Eden's study.

Confusion flooded her mind, surely the breakout of a few orphan boys was not a matter for the police? In the past a number of children had made feeble attempts to leave the orphanage, only to be found days later and returned. The police had never been summonsed in those instances. Millie instinctively knew that there was more to this than just a few boys running away.

Stepping into the back yard she scanned the horizon looking for signs of the boys and men returning from the fields. During the summer months, they were granted a small rest period in the middle of the day. This had always been the time that Millie and James had spent together. She felt both guilty and ungrateful for her behaviour in disobeying Cynthia, whom she adored. She didn't wish to do anything to jeopardise her place at the Rectory, but curiosity told her that there was more to this latest escape than a few runaway boys. She was all too aware of the spiteful Agnes, who she now worked with. Agnes would use any small misdemeanour on Millie's part to have her sent back to the orphanage. However, she absolutely needed to speak to James and see if there was anything they could do to save their young friend and his companions.

She didn't have long to wait. Hungry, dusty and thirsty the group of men and boys appeared as if from nowhere. James, spotting Millie, instantly broke away from the group and led her to a strip of grass away from the open back door.

'Have you heard?' he asked, 'It's terrible, George's a fool, he'll never live after this.'

'I saw the police a moment ago,' Millie whispered. 'What have they done?'

'As far as I know they broke out so I've no idea why the police are here,' answered James with a puzzled look.

'Something is up I know it, The Mistress told me to go straight back home just now, she's never said that before, and she looks worried,' added Millie.

The two siblings were both thinking the same thought. Had George and his friends stolen something before escaping from the orphanage? If that were the case, there would be no mercy from any quarter. There was little time for any further conversation, as James was called inside and Millie was told to leave.

The arrival of the police had been something that The Master had been expecting. After almost every burglary in the neighbourhood an officer of the Law had called at the orphanage to ask if any of its inhabitants were missing or had seen or heard anything unusual. The last statement had always perplexed Mike, as he had often wondered what the rag bag children could have seen or known of a burglary while locked up inside the building! On this day Mike Unwin decided he needed to tread carefully. He wondered what the police knew, and how to play it if he were questioned about the burglary at Eden Manor.

Taking the police officers into Joshua Eden's study, Mike gave an award-winning performance of feigned surprise and disbelief at the burglary of his employer's home. He hastened to ask if Joshua Eden had been informed and even suggested he be excused in order to send a messenger to Nottingham Town immediately to summons his employer home. On being told that the Eden family were on their way home, The Master quickly decided that he would have to confess to allowing four of his charges to run away. In that instant he decided that if there was blame to be placed anywhere, he would put his hands up to the incompetence of Tom. If it came to it, he would insist that Tom was dismissed. He desperately needed an escape route and someone to blame. Tom would serve for now. But what to do about tracking down and bringing to heel George, Ned, Robert and Herbert, not to mention the missing jewellery?

Mike's head throbbed with pain, he swore to himself, that if he got out of this mess, he would never touch a drop of alcohol again. Playing for time he asked if the police had any clues as to who was behind the recent spate of burglaries. To his dismay the police, who up until now had always been talkative, gave little away. He was left feeling decidedly uncomfortable and sorely in need of answers regarding the missing boys and the jewellery. His was a lonely road to tread. His immediate partners in crime were a group of boys no older than 15 who relied on him to advise and protect them. He had to hold his nerve. A search party had been sent out first thing to try to find the four runaways and bring them back to the orphanage.

As he stood and ran through his options, Mike decided he needed to question James Cooper. Something about the boy had always made him feel uneasy, it was as if the boy knew he was a fraud and had little respect for him. When the two children had first arrived at the orphanage, he had taken an instant dislike to both; the sister stood tall and thin with a quiet air of confidence that had made it difficult for him to look her in the eye. The brother too seemed to have the same all-seeing quality. Mike knew that he would have to be careful in his questioning as he didn't want to alert the boy to his real reasons for wanting the gang of runaways returned. A further complication was the sister's elevation to maid at the Rectory. A careless word from him to the boy which might be passed onto the sister could just reach the ear of the Rector and in turn Joshua Eden.

In the meantime, Millie had left the orphanage and returned to the Rectory to find Agnes in a state of excitement. In fact, the silly girl was so excited she forgot to shout at Millie and ask why she hadn't returned earlier.

'The Manor House was robbed last night,' Agnes informed her with glee. 'All their fancy stuff's been nicked, can you believe it!'

'Mr Eden's on his way back now I heard Madam say, can you believe it!' she exclaimed again, her button eyes popping from her head, which darted from side to side as if looking for Joshua Eden to appear in the scullery at any moment.

That was it, Millie thought, but what had the robbery got to do with the runaway boys? Something about it all didn't sit well with her. She hadn't known the other boys at all well, so could not have vouched for their characters, but George had always seemed such a shy, sickly little mite. She found it hard to believe that he would get himself mixed up in a robbery. But then again, he was a little too trusting, and maybe he had simply gone along with whatever plan the other boys had hatched.

'Hey, aint your brother pals with one of them lads that thieved Eden's stuff?'

'What!' exclaimed Millie, her mind racing.

'Don't ya know nowt? Them lads wot broke out of the

orphanage they did the robbery,' Agnes added with glee.

For once she knew more than the clever book-reading girl! She was in her element and was strutting about the room as if she were a court room barrister, cross examining a hapless witness.

'Do ya know what I thinks? I thinks your brother's got a hand in all this stuff. Them orphan lads ain't clever enough to plan a breakout and robbery, but your clever brother could,' she added with a flourish.

Millie's jaw fell open, but no words came out. Inside she was seething. The stupid idiot! If she continued with this sort of talk James, and maybe herself, could be dragged into the whole sorry affair. She would lose her place at the Rectory for sure, if those in high places chose to believe the nonsense Agnes was spouting. Who knows what might happen to James? It took a great deal of self-control for Millie to restrain herself from slapping Agnes's mouth shut.

'Who do you think you are, saying such things about my brother? You don't even know him!' Millie eventually spat back.

Thankfully for Agnes and indeed Millie, at that moment there was a knock at the back door. Both girls, now steaming with rage, rushed to open the door, anything but continue a now very heated argument.

It was the butcher's boy delivering the leg of mutton for the Reverend and Cynthia's dinner.

He too was full of the news. A robbery and four runaway orphan boys who might have committed the robbery. He had never had so much excitement. Kingminster had always seemed such a dull place up until now!

'You're late,' snapped Millie. 'You should have been here this morning. It had better not be off,' she said as she put her nose to the joint of meat to sniff it.

'What's your problem? I was only talking, see ya Agnes,' and without as much as a backward glance he skipped out of the door.

'Don't like the truth do ya?' Agnes snorted and flounced out of the room before Millie had the opportunity to answer.

Thinking it over, James had said nothing about a robbery when she had seen him earlier in the day, did he know? If he did why had he not told her? Was he hiding something? Was he involved and how? The questions came thick and fast, but she found no answers. Poor Millie, she refused to believe that James was in some way connected, but why hadn't he mentioned the robbery?

Whichever way she looked at it, things did not look good. Somehow she needed to see James in private and ask him the questions she was now asking herself. But how, when and where? She had little free time, in fact none. This had never bothered her before, as the only person she wished to spend time with was James, and she saw him once a week.

She knew that she couldn't just leave The Rectory and walk the quarter of a mile to the orphanage and demand to speak to her brother. She had jobs to do that would take up the rest of the day, and she was already behind with her work, due to staying late at the orphanage and the argument with Agnes. Knowing how spiteful Agnes could be, she guessed that she would now be working at a snail's pace so as to leave the bulk of the work to Millie. Millie also had to prepare the vegetables for the evening meal, and light the range, a job which she hated. The ugly range was as temperamental as a cantankerous old woman. If not handled gently it would light, burn for a while and when Millie felt safe to leave it, it would go out! Cynthia's good grace had saved Millie on many an occasion, she had simply laughed and suggested she and The Reverend dine on cold meat and bread. The Reverend had not been so amused, and when Cynthia had been out at one of her morning calls, he had had a stern word with Millie about attending to her jobs diligently. His meaning had been abundantly clear, if she wasn't up to the job she could go back to the orphanage.

How then was she going to get to see James and get to the bottom of the mystery?

By the evening more news had been heard, some truthful, and some fanciful. Cynthia had a visitor who was eager to talk of the despair of the Eden family at being robbed. Knowing she was doing wrong, but feeling she had no choice, Millie had hovered outside the parlour door and listened to snippets of the conversation. The task had not been easy, as she had to listen for movement in the parlour and for movement in the hallway from Agnes. If she had been caught, she was sure that she would have been sent away in disgrace. But Agnes was too busy telling the chimney sweep's boy her views on who had committed the crime. Millie discovered that it was true that a robbery had taken place the previous night at Eden Manor while the family were visiting in Nottingham town and that valuable items of jewellery had been stolen. So far the culprits had not been found.

Agnes seemed to have grown in size. She was now a strutting cock bird, convinced that James Cooper was guilty of the crime, simply through his friendship with one of the runaway boys. Gossip had reached her that four orphan boys had had help to plan and execute their daring crime. It had to be James in her opinion; his sister had been to the Manor a few times along with herself to serve at various parties. Millie could read and write and had possibly drawn a map for her brother of the layout of the house. Ideas were coming thick and fast for Agnes.

'Not long now,' Agnes announced to the empty kitchen. Millie Cooper and her thieving brother would soon be gone.

Chapter 10

News spreads of the robbery 1860

News of the robbery at Eden Manor was on everyone's lips, less so the news of the four runaway boys. Orphans were not considered important enough for the local folk to care about. One person who did care and care very deeply was The Master, Mike Unwin. It had now been two days since that fateful night. He felt as if he had aged 10 years. Joshua Eden was fuming with indignation at having his home violated. He had been heard to say that the culprit or culprits would hang. The newly formed police force in Nottingham town were now under even greater scrutiny than ever before, as Joshua Eden used his influence within the county. After all a new jail had been built in Nottingham to keep the people of the town safe! The police needed to catch the criminals and fast. Mrs Eden was said to be mourning the loss of her diamond and ruby pendant and matching earrings, more than any of her many other items of jewellery.

James had been repeatedly questioned by The Master and had been utterly truthful. He knew nothing of the runaway boys' whereabouts or of their plans. Unfortunately for James The Master did not believe him. Mike Unwin was under increasing pressure from many quarters; his partners in crime were afraid to handle the stolen jewels from Eden Manor in case they were incriminated in some way, so he had had to hide the three jewellery pouches on the premises. His usual practice after a robbery was to saunter down to Nottingham on a matter of business and hand over the jewels to his criminal associates. He always kept a little something from each robbery, as a form of insurance. Much as he was prepared to deal with the Nottingham crooks, he had always felt that he needed a back-up plan, just in case something was to go wrong. He was most unhappy at receiving a message delivered by a ragamuffin boy, telling him to hold onto the jewels until the heat of the robbery had blown over. Keeping them on the premises was risky. Any one of his nosy and disgruntled staff might stumble upon them, and either keep them for themselves or point the finger of guilt at him.

His head seemed to ache daily with all the problems he now had to solve. Where could he hide the jewels that would be safe from detection, and not with his keepsakes? Added to this was the little problem of the diamond and ruby pendant and earrings, which still had not surfaced. If the runaway boys were found with them, could he risk them telling the police how they came to be in their possession? Who would be believed? He thought he might stand a chance of convincing a magistrate that he knew nothing of how the jewellery had ended up outside Joshua Eden's study window, but didn't want to put it to the test. Added to this was an awareness that the orphanage staff had voiced several opinions too close to the truth. His only hope was to find the runaway boys and retrieve the jewels. He would deal with the dirty little thieves once he had the ruby and diamond pendant and matching earrings! Though it pained him he was prepared to hand over the jewels if it got the law off his back. To this end he formulated his plan.

He decided to watch James Cooper and wait to see if he made contact with any of the four. He suspected that George would be missing his close friend and mentor and might try to get in touch. If by the end of the week he had heard nothing, he would have to come up with a way to throw the scent off the orphanage. All could be well as long as they continued to search anywhere but the orphanage. If by chance the police found the runaways and they still had the pendant and earrings he could make the case that they had committed the robbery in the first place and had sold or passed on the rest of the loot. He was convinced he could make a good argument to throw suspicion off himself and onto the hapless Tom. As he sat thinking over his options, he began to feel a modicum of satis-faction: all could still work in his favour.

With his plan in place he continued with his work, taking particular pleasure in thrashing a small boy for working too slowly.

Mike smiled to himself. He liked the idea of throwing Tom to the police as the mastermind behind the robberies. No more burglaries would take place for at least a year or so, to allow things to cool down. He had a tidy sum of money stashed away as his share from previous robberies, as well as a few select pieces of jewellery that he had not wanted to part with. He knew his lads would keep quiet, and hopefully be ready to resume their night-time activities when the time was right, if ever. Running his hand through his thinning hair, Mike felt pleased with himself. Whichever way he looked at it, his plan would ensure that he was never suspected of being involved in any way. Tom, he knew, was too simple to put up much of a fight.

In the meantime, James had continued to work largely alone in the fields. Four boys down meant that the remaining boys had to work even harder. The Master and staff were particular unkind and cruel, and on several occasions, James had found himself struck with The Master's cane for no reason at all. The missing boys had still not surfaced. James hoped that they had managed to escape the clutches of The Master and the harsh regime of the orphanage. By now word had spread amongst the children and staff in the orphanage that Joshua Eden's Manor House had been robbed. The stories grew in daring and cunning with each telling. Some told of the boys shooting one of Joshua Eden's staff. Others how they had stolen one of Mr Eden's fine carriages and horses and ridden away into the night and so the tales went on. All the children and probably a few of the staff wished the runaway boys success. No one doubted for a minute that four poorly educated orphan boys whose ages ranged from 10-14 could have pulled off such a daring crime and disappeared off the face of the earth.

For Millie the robbery and the disappearance of the four boys was a matter of confusion. She could not believe that the two events were connected. She had some, if only a limited knowledge of the boys and knew that that they had not the organisational skills to plan such a crime, or indeed to have been committing robbery for several months undetected. To her it did not add up. There had to be someone older and wiser behind this crime and the previous burglaries. She felt George and his friends were guilty of one crime only. Even then was it a real crime to run away from a cruel and heartless institution?

She had not seen James since Tuesday, the day of the breakout and robbery. Life had carried on as normal in the Rectory, with Agnes goading her, and making snide remarks about 'thieving orphans'. In Agnes's eyes Millie was as guilty as the four boys. The Reverend and Cynthia talked openly about the robbery, and Cynthia had taken to locking her few items of jewellery in a strong box, which she stowed in the top of the wardrobe in their bedroom. This in itself was an inconvenience, as each time she required an item of jewellery, she had to ask Millie to climb into the wardrobe and lift down the heavy box.

The police were no closer to solving the crime, and still hadn't found the four orphan boys. In the village of Kingminster most believed that the four boys had been responsible for the burglary at Eden Manor.

Chapter 11

Mike's plan for James 1860

The Eden family's return to Eden Manor was the talk of Kingminster village. It had been a trying time for the family, and they had not been keen to face the devastation, imagined or otherwise, of the burglary. As it was there was little for them to see or do. The staff had done their best to put the rooms back in order. A display case which had once held a valuable collection of signet rings now stood empty, likewise the jewellery boxes of Mrs Eden and Annabel. One thing which was glaringly obvious was that the thief or thieves knew the real article from paste!

Several beautiful but false items of jewellery had simply been tipped onto the floor or left untouched in their boxes. Both mother and daughter had cried at the loss of their precious jewellery. Joshua Eden had stomped off in search of the local police chief, demanding justice and that the culprit or culprits be caught soon and hung. At this point word had not reached him about the four missing boys from the orphanage. Mike Unwin was in a state of anxiety, with no idea how he was to explain the breakout of four boys and the robbery. He was hoping he could link the two together, but first he had to find the boys. This was not proving to be easy. He knew his only chance of not being linked to the robbery was to retrieve the 'lost' pouch and its contents. Once he had that he would willingly throw the boys to the wolves.

By the Tuesday afternoon Mike had still not heard from Mr Eden; he took this as a good sign. His employer had not made a link between the burglary of his Manor House and the missing boys. This was good, it gave him more time to search for the missing orphans. That morning he had taken a trip into Nottingham town to see a close friend and associate, to ask for his help in the search for the missing boys. He could not risk the staff from the orphanage finding the boys first. A nastier bunch of ruffians that you could ever imagine were now charged with the task of searching the villages and hedgerows around Kingminster village to find the missing boys. Mike had even put up a reward of £1 for the 'associate' who brought back the missing pouch with its contents. He knew that there was little honour amongst thieves. What he did know was he had enough incriminating evidence on the chosen 'associates' to ensure they kept their mouths shut. All he could do now was wait.

But for Mike there was still one fly in his ointment: James Cooper.

'Fetch me Cooper,' he bellowed at no one in particular.

It took some time for James to be brought back from the field and cleaned up sufficiently for an audience with The Master. James was questioned repeatedly about his friendship with George and asked if he had any idea where he and the others could be hiding. Answering truthfully James explained that George had not taken him into his confidence, and he was as mystified as everyone else at his disappearance. Something about The Master's repeated questioning didn't sit well with James. Children had run away before and The Master had never been this concerned. What was he hiding? James had noticed the sweat on the man's top lip and his agitated manner.

He was clearly worried about something and that something was connected to George, Ned, Herbert and Robert.

Mike had eaten a hearty meal, his first since the whole dreadful affair and was beginning to feel a little more like his old self. He had locked himself in his room to inspect the three cotton pouches properly. The lads certainly knew their stuff and had brought him a fine array of jewellery. He was in the process of trying on the many signet rings when there was a knock at the door. Who could it be? He had specifically made it clear to the staff that he was not to be disturbed. Hurriedly pushing the rings back into the pouch, he quickly dropped them into their temporary hiding place. Wiping his eyes as if he had just woken he opened the door to Tom.

'Mr Eden is in the study and he wants to speak to you Sir,' said Tom. 'I didn't dare say you were not to be disturbed,' he added by way of explanation for daring to come anywhere near The Master's rooms. Having carefully shut and locked the door Mike straightened his jacket and headed for Joshua Eden's study. This might have to be his greatest performance to convince his employer of his innocence.

Joshua Eden was not a patient man. Mike found him pacing the room and muttering to himself. The purpose of his visit was soon explained. He had been informed by his butler that several boys had run away from the orphanage. He wondered if Mike knew firstly why any child would wish to leave the care and shelter of such a charitable institution. He also wanted to know what steps Mike had put in place to find the boys and if, as it had been suggested, they were responsible for the robbery of his home. Questions, questions, questions, Mike's head was ringing. He was well aware that Joshua Eden held him responsible for some if not all of what had taken place in his absence. Guile was called for and Mike had that in abundance. In his most charming and oily voice he assured his employer that all was in hand. The boys would be found any day now and would no doubt lead them to the stolen jewellery. Order would be restored, and he had personally overseen the fitting of stouter locks on all the doors and windows. Unwin was dismissed and Joshua Eden turned to leave the orphanage a few minutes later, having inspected a number of the locks on the doors and windows.

Mike Unwin breathed a sigh of relief. That had been close. Joshua Eden did not suspect him in any way, and he intended to keep it that way. But still there was no word on the missing boys. Where could they be hiding and was someone helping them? Thinking this over, the only person he could imagine 'The Halfwit' George turning to would be the Cooper girl, Millie. She had nursed him like a baby when the three children had been brought to the orphanage. He would ask one of his 'associates' to watch the girl and see if George made contact with her. Mike's survival and reputation now rested on finding the lost cotton pouch.

If by the next evening, his associates had not found the missing boys and the jewellery, he would have to revert to plan B. This was trickier and carried an element of risk. The Cooper boy was liked by staff and his fellow orphans. He was hardworking and kind; he was also intelligent and would want to have his say. The later point wasn't too much of a worry for Mike. Magistrates were not usually interested in the testimony of the lower orders. Nevertheless, he had to ensure that the boy was blamed for his part in the robbery and disposed of. Just for a minute and not a second longer Mike Unwin felt a twinge of guilt. James Cooper would most likely hang for a crime he hadn't committed, but there was no other way he could see that would save his own neck. His sleep that night was plagued with images of a shouting mob and the Hang Man's noose!

By the morning Mike's headache had returned, but there was no time for him to worry about his health. Before going to bed he had dispatched a note to his Nottingham friends cum business associates via Charlie the older and more 'trustworthy' of his boys. The essence of the note was to ask for the search to be stepped up and an additional person set to watch Millie Cooper at the Rectory. A time had been set of 10pm for him to meet the leader of the Nottingham associates in The Two Bells public house on Kingminster Lane. For Mike the day seemed to drag. Everywhere he looked he imagined the orphans and staff were judging him. He felt exposed as if there were a hole in his body where his heart might have sat, and all could now see the empty space!

For James the drudgery of life in the orphanage continued. Today he had been told that as they were four boys down, he would have to spend the day spreading horse manure on the fields. He was given no assistance other than a wheelbarrow, a shovel and a rake. The June sun beat down on him and burnt his exposed arms and legs, while the sweat dripped like water off his undernourished body. A stream ran through the grounds of Joshua Eden's estate. James, desperately tired and thirsty, decided he would take the chance of detection and leave his work to go for a drink at the stream. To give the impression of a person at work he pushed the upside-down rake into the ground and draped his torn sweat soaked shirt over it. Lastly, he placed an upturned bucket on top. It wasn't a good scarecrow and would easily have been detected if anyone looked close enough, but he didn't care. From a distance he hoped that any boy or staff member glancing towards the upper fields would see a person standing in the field. It would hopefully give him enough time to wander down to the stream for a much-deserved drink and rest.

Satisfied with his scarecrow James set off in the burning sun in the direction of the stream. He was soon drinking the cool clear water and splashing his sun-burnt body. He was so absorbed in the cooling pleasure of the water, that he was unaware of a small figure creeping up behind him. The sound of a twig breaking made him turn sharply. He half expected to feel a blow from a cane as one of the staff beat him for his negligence. Instead to his surprise he saw the wide moon face of Ned.

'Ned, mate, where have you been hiding? They're out looking for you lads everywhere.'

'It's bad James, we didn't nik owt, but we'll be blamed,' blurted out Ned. Understandably he was agitated, but James was not following what he was saying.

'What do you mean, you didn't nik owt?' asked James.

It suddenly began to dawn on him why The Master had been so cross. The burglary at Eden Manor was the work of the four runaways! The Master would be angry, as the boys were in his charge. Their actions would reflect badly on him. But something wasn't right. Could the four undernourished waifs really have been daring enough to break into Eden Manor? James very much doubted this.

'Honest James, it was George, he tripped over it and just picked it up and we all ran,' urged Ned.

He could see that James was thinking hard, Ned was desperate to clear his name and those of his fellow friends if only to another orphan.

'You're not making sense Ned, I'm not with you, tell me quick what happened,' James asked while glancing furtively around them.

He knew the static scarecrow wouldn't fool those working

in the lower field for long and soon someone might come looking for him.

Ned quickly explained how they had escaped through Mr Eden's study window, and how George had twisted his ankle when he landed awkwardly. In no time at all James saw the full picture. The boys would be blamed for the robbery and all would undoubtedly hang. But what he couldn't understand was why Mrs Eden's jewels had come to be outside the study window in the first place.

'Where's the stuff now Ned?'

'George has it, he's got to get it back to the orphanage or the house, so we can be in the clear, we're not thieves James you believe me don't ya?' pleaded Ned.

James believed him but doubted if others would. The real thief or thieves would be glad to see someone else take the blame for their crime. So, where did The Master fit into this? He was obviously very angry, angrier than most about the four boys' disappearance. Did he know who had committed the burglary?

'I've got to get back Ned, we don't want us both being flogged,'

'I'm sorry James, I hope I see you again, but if I'm caught you will speak up for me won't you mate?' Ned added as tears ran down his face leaving streaks in the dirt.

The two boys parted. Luckily for James no one had missed him, as they were all too busy with their heads bent low to avoid the burning sun. Back at his post James thought over what Ned had told him. He could tell no one, there was no one in the orphanage he could trust with such a secret. He needed to speak to his clever younger sister Millie. She had always been able to see the full picture in any scenario. He would have to find a way to see her and soon, before her next visit to the orphanage on the following Tuesday. Hours later James heard the whistle which signalled that work in the field was over.

Back in the orphanage James knew that there would be no opportunity for him to get a message to Millie. The staff had strict instructions to lock the doors and windows once the day's work had been completed. Mrs Peabody, The Rector's wife could be heard talking to The Master though the open dining room cum workroom door. She often visited at mealtimes as she wished to ensure the children were eating a nourishing meal. James longed to rush from the room and tell her what he had learnt from Ned, but he knew that as soon as he stood up, he would be challenged for his insubordination and punished. He wondered if he would ever get the opportunity to tell Ned's tale. There had to be another way. He had heard the staff talking about the search that was taking place for the four boys whom all believed to have committed the burglary at Eden Manor. It was only a matter of time until the boys were found. Where could they be hiding? Thankfully it was hot, so they would not have to worry about keeping warm.

After dinner the children continued to work inside the building. At long last the working day was finally over. Tom, who supervised the boys' dormitory, had taken to locking himself inside the dormitory whilst the boys prepared for bed. The Master had been particularly hard on him after the four boys had run away. He seemed to bear a grudge; as if Tom had been responsible for the actions of the four. Prayers said and overtired from the heat and their labours the boys settled down to sleep.

Downstairs all was not so calm; Mike's head was buzzing and he could hardly keep still. The police had called again asking how the search was going. He obviously had no news to give them and hadn't liked the tone of the sergeant's voice. Having ensured that all the children were accounted for, he left for his meeting at The Two Bells public house on Kingminster Lane. There was nothing untoward about his behaviour. His sister Jane lived over the pub and worked behind the bar. He too had often been seen drinking with a group of rough men in the public house. Tonight, as he and his companion sat in the small snug, the pub was almost empty so there were few to overhear their conversation.

'Well?' he asked by way of greeting.

'Nowt mate, not a word, they've disappeared and taken the loot with 'em,' replied his companion.

'Keep looking, and watch the girl at the Rectory, they may try to pass her something so be ready,' Mike added as he raked his hand through his greasy thinning hair.

'Looks like I'm going to have to make something happen, it might flush them out,' he added as he rose, drained his glass and left the pub.

Back in his room Mike took a lingering look at the contents of the three pouches before placing them in their hiding place. He was uneasy about keeping them on the premises but at present he had no choice. Tomorrow would be the day!

Chapter 12

The Attic Room 2019

Lewis and Lupin spent the remainder of the afternoon cycling around the village of Kingminster. Lupin pointed out the main features of the village; namely the school and the village store, Lewis had already seen the church as he lived next door to it. The beauty and splendour of Eden Manor House made Lewis stop and stare. Set back from the road and protected by a stone wall it stood proud and imposing in the Nottinghamshire countryside. Lupin wasn't able to tell him much about the current Eden family apart from the fact that the family originally owned most of the village, and that the Edens occasionally paid a visit to the school on Prize Day and sometimes for Sports Day, but apart from that she had seen very little of them.

'Me Dad says the Edens must be broke, that's why they're selling the orphanage, but I think it's a good idea to turn it into a hotel. Mum said Mr Eden has told the village that we can use the gym and swimming pool at a discounted rate,' smiled Lupin.

She had a beautiful open face, and her smile seemed to come up from the tips of her toes to the top of her head. Lewis smiled too, but he didn't know why. Perhaps he was just happy to have made such a lovely new friend. She was certainly very different to the gaggle of friends he had left behind in London.

As Lewis stood admiring Eden Manor he thought of his father. He hadn't been in touch with him that day, despite their promise to message every day. His life was moving on and, little did he know it, but it was soon to change in a most spectacular way.

The distance from the Manor House to the orphanage was no more than half a mile. A short cut could be taken across the fields that surrounded the two buildings. Taking out his phone, Lewis took a number of pictures of the Manor House and the old orphanage. He had told his mum he would be back by 3 o'clock, it was now 4 and she hadn't phoned. That in itself was a good sign; she must be feeling safe and knew he would be happy in Lupin's company. Lewis decided to phone his mum and ask if he could stay out even longer. It was a beautiful summer's day, the sun shone brightly making everything look clean and fresh. A gentle breeze stirred the trees and hedgerows. To his surprise his mum agreed to his request, she told him that she had given up on the unpacking and was now attacking a few of the many weeds in the garden.

Lupin suggested they head back to her grandparents' house and use their computer to find out more about James Cooper. Lewis thought this a brilliant idea. He had not wanted to tell her that he had already compiled a list of things he wanted to research about the deserted orphanage and The Old Rectory. It felt good that here was a new friend who was interested in the same things as himself. Back at Mr and Mrs Featherstone's house Lupin explained what they had planned to do. Her granddad thought it a good idea and even offered to help, but Lupin was having none of it!

'Gramps, you're too slow on the computer. Just leave it to us please,' she said flashing him one of her winning smiles.

It worked; the two children settled down in the front room where the computer was set up on a corner table complete with its own tablecloth and a crocheted smaller cloth placed under the mouse!

Lupin and Lewis discovered that James Cooper had been 14 years old at the time of his trial in Nottingham Town in September 1860. Having watched many crime dramas featuring a trial both children were surprised to read that no one had represented James at his. He had been treated as an adult, found guilty of the robbery at Eden Manor and disappeared.

'It doesn't say what happened to him, do you think he was hung?' asked Lewis. He felt sad for the boy and wondered how he would have felt to be all alone in the world.

'It says here that no one attended on his behalf,' Lupin added. 'But I thought he had a sister, the girl called Millie?'

'Perhaps girls weren't allowed to go to court in those days,' said Lewis. 'The Victorians were a strange lot and very goody two shoes,' he added in his best prim and proper voice.

Lupin laughed but seemed to take on board what Lewis had said.

'Can you believe this happened here in our city and village over a hundred and fifty years ago?' Lewis added.

Lupin looked up from the computer screen and smiled.

'Our city eh? I suppose it is now you live in Nottingham-shire, hey up me duck!' she laughed as Lewis squirmed in his seat.

Lewis eventually left the warm stuffy room to cycle home to The Old Rectory. Mum had been out and had bought food. The smell of roast chicken drifted to his nostrils as he opened the back door.

'I take it you've had a good day Mr Woo, you look more like old self.'

'So do you Mum.'

Slipping into the kitchen through the scullery and averting

his eyes from old range, Lewis felt happier than he had felt for days. His parents had sprung their divorce on him at the last minute and the move had all been planned without a word to him. He was still cross at his parents for that, after all he wasn't a baby! But Lupin and her grandparents had made him feel so welcome and part of their small community and that was wonderful. Lewis had always enjoyed History at school. Now here he was in a village with an interesting past and indeed living in the house of someone connected to the famous James Cooper. Heading up to his bedroom he made a quick call to his dad and had what he would call a 'nothing' conversation. Dad seemed happy just to hear his son's voice and asked lots of questions which Lewis did his best to avoid answering.

Sitting down to dinner Lewis and his mum were happily joking with one another on how Lewis had already started to use one or two Nottingham phrases. They were interrupted by a knock at the front door. It immediately put a stop to their banter. Mum gave a quick appraising glance around the kitchen before she hastened towards the door. Lewis could hear her laughing and talking happily to another woman. Curiosity got the better of him and putting down his knife and fork he left the table and followed his mother into the hall. She was leading the woman towards the kitchen. Their visitor was roughly the same age as his mum and looked strangely familiar, on seeing Lewis standing by the kitchen door the woman's face broke into a warm smile.

'Lupin,' Lewis muttered.

'Lewis, this is Lupin's Mum Mrs Anderson,' his Mum informed him. Lewis grinned, he was right.

'Sally, please, I only get called Mrs Anderson on important occasions,' laughed Sally Anderson.

She had the same cheering smile as her daughter, Lewis liked her instantly. She held out a bottle of wine and passed a square sweet tin to Lewis. Inside was homemade fudge. How had she known that this was his favourite?

'Dinner first, young man,' Mum added, with a wink.

'I see you're eating so I'll leave you to it, but why don't you and Lewis come over to ours on Saturday for a drink and meet Matt my husband. Shall we say 7? I'll even lay on some snacks.'

And with that she left.

'Well what a friendly place! I told you, you would like Nottingham!' Mum said as she put the bottle of wine on the dresser, and firmly put the lid back on the tin of fudge which she also placed on the dresser.

By bedtime Lewis and mum had finally decided on a day and time to collect Truffle. They made plans to go into Nottingham the following morning to buy dog food and other essentials. Lewis had pared his list of dog necessities down considerably. A phone call to The Featherstones had been made to ensure that the correct dog food was purchased; everything else was up to them.

Bathed and ready for bed Lewis kissed his mum goodnight. She was definitely looking happier. He too was feeling pretty good. She had managed to finish the unpacking in his room. Some items he would re-arrange, but she hadn't made a bad job of finding homes for his games and books. She had even re-positioned the computer table under the window, which gave him a perfect view of the surrounding countryside, and the old orphanage. As he clicked through his messages he glanced out of the window. It was not quite dark, and the screen acted as a form of mirror. He could see his own reflection staring at the screen, but behind him was someone else. Turning sharply and nearly wrenching his neck Lewis was in time to see the back of a figure run from the room. This was no coincidence, someone or something was watching him. He guessed that whoever it was, whether it be living or dead would have headed for the attic rooms. Swallowing down the bile that was now in his throat he leapt from the chair and ran to follow the fleeting figure. He quickly flicked the switch at the bottom of the landing which led to the attic and climbed the stairs.

The landing revealed nothing. Neither did the smaller of the rooms. Pushing open the larger bedroom door, Lewis found himself perplexed at the change in the once cold and unwelcoming room. The air felt warm, the light brighter and the grate looked as if someone had cleaned it. Perhaps mum had been up to the room and made a start at trying to make it more habitable? Somehow, Lewis knew this was not the case. At dinner when he had once again mentioned the neglected attic rooms, mum had told him that they were very low on her list of priorities. He was to ignore them, as she was doing, until they had the rest of the house in a more orderly condition. Turning to leave Lewis realised that the door had shut behind him. He had most certainly left it open, in fact he had pushed it wide open. The door was firmly closed. Fear filled his mind. Whatever was happening was beginning to unnerve him.

'Stop it!' he shouted to no one in particular.

The door handle refused to turn. It reminded him of the games he had played when younger with Alfie his best friend in London. Alfie used to enjoy holding a door tightly shut making it impossible for him to get out of a room. The presence of the person on the other side was real, but this was no game, Lewis was definitely feeling afraid.

'Mum, Mum help me!' he shouted, but there was no answer. She was probably fast asleep in her bedroom on the landing below and had not heard him through the thick walls.

'What do you want?' he shouted 'Who are you? Is it Millie?'

The mention of the name worked and the grip on the other side of the door was gone, the door swung open and Lewis was free to leave the attic room, but he didn't.

'Stand up to bullies,' dad had always told him, 'even if you're afraid don't let them see it.'

But something about the atmosphere in the room told him he was not being bullied. Something or someone was trying to communicate with him. Whatever that was it had to be connected to the attic bedroom. He had taken on board the Featherstones' comments about the house being haunted and had wondered what his mum would have said if he told her. She was happy again. So was he, despite the ugly range and the pokey attic rooms. He could live with them if they left him alone.

The atmosphere in the room changed again. Lewis no longer felt afraid. Instead a feeling of deep sadness seemed to wrap itself around him and fill the empty room. The feeling was akin to how he had felt when his parents had told him they were going to divorce. It was a sadness of loss, emptiness and despair.

'What do you want, tell me please?' he pleaded to the empty room.

There was nothing, no movement, no noise, no change in atmosphere. It was as if the 'invisible person' were holding his or her breath. Feeling that he was getting nowhere, Lewis shrugged his shoulders and left the room. Switching off the light he pulled the door firmly shut behind him. Back on the main landing Lewis put his head around his mum's bedroom door to check that she was okay. She was fast asleep curled up on her side, snoring gently. Feeling reassured he went into his own room. Without making a noise he purposefully shut the door firmly behind himself. As he sat on the edge of his bed, he realised that he was shaking. Maybe the house was wrong for them after all? Who would want to live with a ghost?

After what seemed an age Lewis finally fell asleep. That night he dreamt that he was at school, but not his old school in London, but an old Victorian building. Everyone was in Victorian costume; it must have been a dressing up day. There were no white boards or computers and the desks were old and made of wood with ink wells. Slate tablets were on each desk and the children were copying the alphabet from a large blackboard at the front of the classroom. One girl sat quietly staring out of the window. Her slate was blank. The clothes of the pupils were rough and misshaped, some of the girls looked in need of a wash, but not this particular girl. Her clothes were old, and had been carefully patched and mended, but they were clean, as were her face, hands and boots.

'Millie Cooper pay attention!' called the teacher, a beautiful woman finely dressed and with elegant long fingers, which she tapped continuously on the desk in front of her.

The girl called Millie gazed with blank eyes at the teacher. Tears ran down her checks.

'I'm thinking of James Miss, I'm sorry Miss but I can't help it.' sobbed the girl. 'Who's going to help him now?' she added.

Lewis woke in a sweat, James and Millie Cooper again!

The next morning, Lewis and mum prepared to visit the City of Nottingham. Lewis had only ever visited Nottingham as a small boy, when his gran had been alive, so had no memories of the shopping centre and its sites. It was enormous, with every type of imaginable shop. They were able to find all they needed in one large pet shop on the outskirts of the city. With the car loaded Lewis asked mum if they could take a look around the old Lace Market. His computer search had informed him that back in the 1860's Nottingham Shire Hall, which was now a museum, had been the court in which all local trials had taken place.

The building was now called The National Justice Museum. Mum was curious at Lewis's choice but decided to go along with it, after all anything to make him feel a connection with Nottingham was good. Had she known his real intention she might not have been so keen. On the pavement outside The Old Shire Hall, Lewis tried to imagine what it must have been like for James, a boy not much older than himself. Convicted of burglary and theft, his guilt confirmed. Lewis doubted that the boy could have broken into the Manor House and stolen the large number of jewels that he had read about as stolen from the Victorian Joshua Eden. Admittedly the reports of the crime had said the boy had accomplices, but he had never given up the names of any of these. Maybe he had been part of a gang, and had been too afraid of the others to implicate them? But this didn't add up. He was at the time in the orphanage, so why had Mr Eden, the police and magistrate been so eager to believe he was guilty? Turning from the building Lewis felt uncomfortable and sad; he was beginning to feel a connection to James and Millie Cooper.

'Thanks Mum, we don't have to go inside, I just wanted to see the place up close.'

He had decided that he would not enter the building with his mum, or indeed at all until he had done some more research. Millie's presence in The Old Rectory, seemed to be urging him on to find something. Looking puzzled mum simply followed her son back out of the Lace Market to the car park.

Once home, the dog items together with the rest of the shopping were unpacked. Lewis excused himself and went up to the attic room. He wanted to think. In the cold light of day, the room was once again icy cold and sad. It wasn't long before he felt the presence of someone or something. The room felt warmer and more welcoming, somehow. Lewis got the distinct feeling he was being watched. The door remained open, he had made sure of this by bringing a book with him, to use as a door wedge. Nothing happened, perhaps the ghost was bidding her time. By now Lewis was sure that Millie Cooper was the ghost. It had been the same girl he had seen in his room, the coal house and in his dreams. If he could find out the truth about James, she might just leave him alone!

Chapter 13

Truffle 2019

At last the day had come for Lewis and his mum to collect the puppy. Lewis had hardly slept the night before. All thoughts of James Cooper were now put to the back of his mind. He had a real live puppy to occupy his thoughts. Millie also seemed to have quietened down and had stopped plaguing his dreams. He was totally engrossed in making the house comfortable for his new puppy. Mum had drawn the line at the suggestion that Truffle slept in his room. The crate was set up in the old scullery, much to Lewis's annoyance. He pointedly moved it over to the window away from the ugly black range.

'She can look out at the garden,' he had explained when mum had asked why he had moved the crate.

'She won't be able to see out of the window Lewis, it's too high up,' added mum with a grin. Sometimes her son was a mystery to her.

'Being close to the range would mean she will be warm in the winter. Why do you skirt round it as if it's going to bite you?' she added.

Ignoring his mum Lewis turned his attention to the garden. The back door had been left open to allow air to circulate in the warm kitchen and scullery. Was it his imagination or had he just seen a figure enter the coal house? Lewis shot out of the scullery and turned the handle on the coal house door. It was locked! Going back into the house he found the keys and went to open the door. He now knew exactly where to find the light switch, and he turned on the light. He took his time in looking around the small room. Nothing seemed to be out of place. But once again he felt the presence of another person.

'Millie please tell me what you want me to do?' he asked.

The air was silent, Lewis held his breath. His instincts told him that someone or something was present in the cramped space. Not knowing which way to turn he stood stock still in anticipation. A loud rattling sound accompanied by a grinding noise shattered the silence of the room, making Lewis jump. Still holding his breath, he realised the noise was coming from the central heating boiler in the corner. Letting out his breath he reasoned to himself that his mum must have turned it on. After all, what other explanation could there be? Reaching for the door handle Lewis held it firmly as he took one final backwards glance around the dirty confined space. Once safely in the kitchen he took a minute to compose himself. Mum had taken to watching his face too closely these days and had probably sensed that something was spooking him. With his back to his mother Lewis stood at the kitchen window looking out at the bird table.

'Did you just turn the boiler on Mum?' he asked, but even before she had given her answer he knew that she would answer in the negative.

'Don't be daft son, it's boiling outside and in, why would I do such a thing?'

She turned to check the boiler control on the wall next to the range. Satisfying herself that all was normal she gave Lewis a quizzical look and left the room.

With his heart pounding Lewis stepped out of the kitchen

through the scullery and once more entered the coal house. The noise from the boiler had stopped, but now on the floor was a small pile of brick dust, as if someone had been drilling a hole in the red brick wall. He could have sworn it hadn't been there earlier. Perhaps the boiler coming on had shaken it loose? The explanation didn't satisfy him. It was clear that Millie was back and had something to say. So why didn't she just tell him straight out or write it down? He made a mental note of the room and thinking better of it went to fetch his phone. The battery was flat. He told himself that he must remember to put it to charge each evening, but he had been saying this since he had first been given a mobile phone a few years previously. He would talk to Lupin when they went to collect the puppy and ask her what she thought was the significance of the brick dust. He didn't hold out much hope that she would be able to advise him, but he liked the idea of them having a shared secret.

It had been decided that mother and son would walk Truffle home, so with the new collar and lead they set off to walk the short distance to the Featherstones' house. Passing the orphanage Lewis stared hard at the upstairs windows. There was no sign of life or movement. Both James and Millie had once slept in one of the rooms, and Millie was now trying to tell him something.

On reaching the Featherstones' house, all thoughts of James and Millie vanished from Lewis's mind. Truffle must have known that today was a special day. She bounded across the kitchen and gave a brilliant impression of a kangaroo! Lewis couldn't help smiling at his little cockapoo puppy. She continually jumped and yelped until he had sat down in the high-backed chair and she was on his lap licking his face. A feeling of wellbeing and satisfaction came over him, as he laughed and stroked her beautiful soft coat. After what seemed an age of tea drinking and much eating of cakes, Lewis, mum and Lupin left the house to walk back to The Old Rectory. Lupin had sensed that Lewis wanted to talk to her in private. Once they were back in the house and the puppy was exploring her new garden, she asked him why he had looked so worried earlier on.

'I think James Cooper's sister Millie is haunting me,' he whispered as they stood on the patio watching Truffle sniffing the ground and rushing from one spot to another.

'What's happened now?' asked Lupin.

Lewis quickly explained all that had taken place since he had found the old newspaper.

'I'm not sure I would like to live in a house with a ghost,' mused Lupin. Seeing Lewis's face drop she quickly added, 'But, it's an adventure, perhaps we could try and find out what she wants from you and once we find it she might leave you alone.'

That was it! Lewis had been hoping she would make such a suggestion, after all Mrs Drew, his teacher, had often said 'two heads were better than one'.

Truffle seemed satisfied with her exploration of her new garden, so Lewis suggested that they show her the rest of the house. Mum had insisted that she was either carried or put on the lead for the viewing, as she had noticed the pup's tendency to pick up and chew anything that looked or smelt interesting. Putting the lead back on the pup, Lewis and Lupin began their tour. Truffle wagged her tail enthusiastically as they went from room to room. Upstairs in Lewis's bedroom she had tried to jump onto the bed. She was very curious at Lewis's shelf of soft toys especially the toy birds. Reluctantly they climbed the stairs to the attic rooms. Once on the upper landing the puppy's behaviour changed; she began to whimper and pulled Lewis towards the larger of the two rooms.

'I told you there's something going on up here,' Lewis whispered to Lupin, although there was no one there apart from themselves and Truffle.

Pushing open the door the two children stepped into the main attic bedroom. Immediately Truffle began straining at the lead, pulling Lewis towards the window. Her actions were not those of a frightened dog, but rather those of one encountering a familiar friend with whom she was keen to get reacquainted.

'Millie,' whispered Lupin and Lewis together.

Both children held their breath. The puppy continued to bark and pull. Taking a step further into the room Lewis found himself trying to restrain the little dog as she yanked at her lead in an attempt to reach whatever had caught her attention at the window. Neither Lewis nor Lupin could see anything in the room. As Lewis let the puppy pull him over to the window, both children were amazed to watch the puppy sit and wag her tail as if she were being stroked by an invisible hand.

'Dogs can see ghosts,' Lupin breathed. 'She's not afraid, look at her.'

It was true. Truffle appeared happy and playful, wagging her tail and then jumping up in her customary kangaroo fashion. The room remained silent, but gone was the cold and intimidating atmosphere. Lewis was later to have said it was as if the ghost had accepted them all.

Turning to leave the room Lewis found Truffle was unwilling to leave. The little dog had to be dragged from the room. Millie had not spoken, but neither had she seemed displeased. Once downstairs and in the back garden, Truffle was let off the lead and allowed to continue her exploration of the garden. Fetching the key to the coal house, Lewis turned the lock slowly and opened the door. He had explained to Lupin the images, whether real or imagined, of Millie in the coal house. He turned on the dim light bulb, both children stood and looked around the dusty room. Nothing out of the ordinary was detected, and both jumped as Truffle nudged the door further open and began to explore the small dirty space.

As Lewis glanced around the room, he noticed immediately that the small pile of brick dust had gone. Had his mum been into the coal house and swept it up? He didn't think so, so who had cleaned it up and why?

'I'm going mad,' Lewis wailed. Both Lupin and Truffle turned to stare at him. Confusion clouded Lupin's pretty face.

'What's up Lewis?' she asked.

'The brick dust that was over there has gone!' he exclaimed as he pointed to the far wall.

Lupin stared at the floor and tried to make sense of what Lewis was saying. She felt uncomfortable as she could clearly see that he was distressed, but she did not know how to console him.

'Let's ask your Mum,' she suggested, and purposefully turned to leave the room.

'No.' cried Lewis. 'She'll probably ground me and hide the key if she thinks I'm imagining things.'

'Who else has been in your house?' asked Lupin, now trying to find a logical explanation to appease Lewis.

'No one but you, me, Mum and Millie,' he added trying to make light of the situation.

He could see from Lupin's face that she was worried. He didn't want to scare away his only friend. After all she barely knew him. She might think he was strange, apt to fantasise and making things up to seek attention.

'Let's just leave it for now,' he added, and with his shoulders slumped he turned towards the door shooing the puppy out onto the patio.

Lupin shook her head in disbelief and followed Lewis out of the dark confined space. Being a smart and sensitive girl, she knew that it was best to leave this conversation where it was and give Lewis time to calm down. She honestly believed his explanation. Not for one second did she believe that his mum had been into the coal house and swept up a small pile of brick dust. After all if she had why hadn't she swept up the coal dust and gravel that was strewn across the coalhouse floor? Mrs Henry didn't look the sort of woman to do half a job!

As the two children stood on the patio watching Truffle chase after a blackbird, then turn to try and chase her own tail, conversation seemed stilted. Lewis felt stupid and embarrassed at his outburst, and poor Lupin didn't know what to say as reassurance. Their silence was broken by Mrs Henry calling the children inside. Both turned to enter the house, glad of a distraction. Truffle, seeing her playmates go indoors, followed.

'What were you doing in the coal house?' mum asked.

'Just showing Lupin the house Mum,' replied Lewis unable to make eye contact with either his mum or Lupin.

'Well there's nothing to see in there is there?' mum laughed. 'I haven't been in the place since I viewed the house months ago,' she added as she took the key from Lewis and hung it on its peg.

'I thought I just heard my phone ping, Lupin, shall we put the laptop on and see if we can message my old school friends?'

And with that Lewis rushed from the kitchen and took the stairs two at a time. Lupin followed. Mrs Henry had given both children the confirmation they needed. Lewis wasn't going mad, neither was he imagining things, something or someone had created the brick dust and had now swept it up! But why? What was its significance?

Chapter 14

A Beating 1860

The warm sunlight drifted through the thin shutters into the sparse and unloved dormitory. Turning over in his cot bed to avoid the light, James thought of George who had occupied the bed to his right, which was now empty. He wondered where George was and if he was alright. George was sickly and needed guidance. James hoped that the other boys were looking after him, he was far too trusting of others. James knew that if George were caught with Mrs Eden's jewels he would probably hang or die a slow death in some rat-infested prison. Despite his small stature and weak frame, James felt that a judge might just believe that George and the other boys had been responsible for the robbery at Eden Manor. The sound of the key turning in the lock signalled that it was time to rise. Tom shook the bell with such force that he could have woken the dead! James stirred from his contemplation and throwing off the scratchy thin blanket joined the other boys at the basins to wash and prepare for yet another day of hard labour in the burning sun.

Breakfast was the same thin watery porridge. Indeed, James had often joked with George that as the week went on the porridge seemed to get thinner! Having eaten their meal, each of the boys fell into a series of lines depending on their work duties for that week. James always seemed to be assigned to the fields, and today was no exception. With his tools and barrow, he headed out into the lower field to dig up carrots. This was a pleasant change from shovelling horse manure. It also gave him the chance to eat the odd carrot when no one was looking. Any sort of additional food was always welcome to the near starved orphans.

He had barely begun to work when he spotted the figure of The Master coming towards him. Now James had given considerable thought to the brief conversation he had with Ned the previous day. Something told him that The Master's interest in the four orphan boys was not for their safety but was most likely connected to the burglary at Eden Manor. James was convinced that Mr Unwin knew something about the break-in at Eden Manor. Since the robbery The Master had questioned James repeatedly asking the same questions about the whereabouts of George and the others. His preoccupation with the four runaways was unnatural. He had never taken such a keen interest in any of the previous children who had run away from the orphanage. So why George, Ned, Herbert and Robert? James had concluded that it had something to do with the jewels that George had literally stumbled upon. The Master must have known they were missing, but how would he have known that? Surely Mr Eden would not have discussed the exact details or indeed any details of the robbery with the manager of his orphanage?

Thinking back, he remembered over-hearing snippets of conversations between staff about other local robberies. They had been indignant at being questioned by the overly zealous police force after any burglary in the neighbourhood had taken place. They had grumbled loudly about how any of them could have committed the crimes when they were all locked up at nights in the orphanage. Piecing it all together James felt sure that The Master knew something about the previous robberies and this current robbery at Eden Manor. After all, if what he had heard from Tom and other staff members was true, The Master was the only inhabitant of the orphanage who could come and go as he wished. Added to this were the times when some of the boys were supposedly being 'punished' and did not appear in the dormitory until the following morning. It all had to be connected in some way, but how was he to find out and who could he tell?

'Cooper, here now boy!' bellowed The Master.

Putting down his fork James brushed himself down. The dry clay soil had embedded itself deep into the ridges of his calloused hands. Taking a minute to collect his thoughts James walked slowly towards Mike Unwin. What was happening now? Had George and the others been found? Somehow, he had to get a message to Millie, he desperately needed to share his thoughts with the one person in this world whom he could trust. Following The Master James was led into the workroom where the younger boys and the girls worked on menial tasks. To James's surprise and joy there was Millie, Agnes and Mrs Peabody. Keeping his eyes to the ground James tried to look glum. He could feel the button eyes of Agnes boring into him and was determined to give nothing away. The whole situation was definitely out of the ordinary and for a moment he wondered if it was some sort of trap.

'Ah James, Millie tells me you love gardening, The Reverend is in need of some additional help at The Rectory and Millie has suggested you,' blurted Cynthia Peabody, avoiding James's gaze and glancing instead at Mike Unwin for confirmation.

'I've had a word with Mr Unwin, and he has said he can spare you for the day, so come along, look sharp, lots of digging and planting for you to do and no time to waste.'

James found himself free to leave the orphanage if only for a day. Outside the front door, Mrs Peabody got into her carriage and the three young people were left to make their way back to the Rectory on foot.

As the carriage swept out of the orphanage through the iron gates, the three children hurried to keep up. Once outside the gates James and Millie hugged one another much to the disgust of Agnes. A look passed between the brother and sister which made Agnes shrug her shoulders and stomp on ahead of the pair. Not a word was said, James held Millie's hand and they walked in silence the quarter of a mile down Kingminster Lane to The Rectory on Church Lane. Both were overjoyed at being together again, and both had so much to tell the other, but that would have to wait until they were out of earshot of the nosy Agnes.

At the Rectory James was met by the Rector and his gardener. Reverend Peabody did not seem pleased to see James and dismissed him with a wave of his hand, telling him to speak to his gardener regarding his duties for the day. James was soon set to work digging over a neglected border at the bottom of the garden which had become overgrown with nettles and every weed imaginable. Glancing up the garden to the house James could just make out the top of Millie's head at the scullery window. After several long hours of digging, James was covered from head to toe in the seed from the chickweed. He had been stung repeatedly by nettles. His body was dripping with sweat and he longed for a drink of water. Once again looking towards the scullery in hope, James saw Millie stepping out of the back door with a plate and mug in her hands. It was lunch time at last. The gardener had disappeared into the house to eat his lunch with Agnes in the kitchen. Knowing they had little time to talk James quickly told

Millie what had taken place at the orphanage since that fateful Monday night. He explained his thoughts on the involvement of The Master, but in what capacity he could not tell. Millie's face clouded over with fear when James told her of his brief conversation with Ned.

'Do you think the boys are innocent?' she asked.

'I do, I think someone else did the robbery and they accidentally found some of the stolen jewellery.' replied James.

'What's going to happen now?' asked Millie

'I don't know, but The Master's involved I'm sure. He's asked me no end of questions about where I think the boys are hiding and was I part of their gang.'

'Strange, why would he ask you such questions? You don't know anything do you James?' whispered Millie.

'No, I don't, but something ain't right. Tell no one what I've told you and keep your...'

Their conversation was interrupted by none other than Agnes who had crept up on the pair eager to eavesdrop on their furtive conversation.

'Like a pair of thieves you two, what's the whispering about?' snorted Agnes. 'You're needed in the 'ouse,' she snapped at Millie.

'And you're here to work so get on wi' it,' she added as she looked James up and down and decided she didn't like what she saw.

Back in the kitchen Millie ran through what James had told her. Things looked bad for George and his friends, but what could she do or say to make a difference? Perhaps if she talked to The Mistress and told her what she knew, she might see a way of helping the runaway boys. But James had told her to keep quiet. She wasn't sure how the beautiful mistress would be able to help even if she believed her story. Millie very much doubted that Reverend Peabody would be willing to help the four boys, particularly if it involved him going against Mr Eden.

'Best to keep quiet,' she muttered to herself, but she wasn't satisfied or happy with that option.

The remainder of the day passed without incident. By dusk James had cleared the border and had planted many of the cuttings that the gardener had placed outside the back door. Preparing to leave, James assumed he would simply walk back to the orphanage. However, he was told by the gardener that he was to wait in the back yard. Collecting his shirt, he popped his head around the back door and said goodbye his sister. The gardener was now standing in front of the closed garden gate as if he were a guard. James thought nothing of the strange behaviour and stood admiring the beautiful roses.

'I can walk back by myself you know, I'm hardly likely to run off!' James said to the gardener who was now looking decidedly uncomfortable.

Something wasn't right. Perhaps The Master was afraid he too would run away and join the others. The thought of this made him smile. But his joke was short lived. The sound of voices and heavy boots running towards the garden gate signalled the arrival of The Master accompanied by Tom and the local constable. The Reverend and his wife were conspicuously absent, as the constable announced that he was arresting James for his involvement in the burglary and theft at Eden Manor.

Agnes, Millie and the gardener all stood and watched in amazement as James was handcuffed and led away. Millie tried to run to her brother but was restrained by Agnes, who was most definitely having the time of her life.

'Thieving scum,' she breathed into Millie's face as she pulled the frantic girl back into the house.

In a flash, James was gone and there was nothing that

Millie could do but cry. Neither brother nor sister had seen this coming. Both had thought that they might have to speak up for George, Ned, Robert and Herbert, but had not thought for one moment that James would be implicated in the crime, if it was a crime to run away from slavery. Millie tried hard to fathom how James could be accused of being involved in the break-in at Eden Manor! This had to be a mistake, or was James right and The Master was pushing the blame onto him to draw attention away from himself?

All this and more rushed through Millie's head as she stood restrained by Agnes and watching her brother being dragged into the waiting police wagon. Back in the house there was still no sign of The Reverend and Cynthia Peabody. Both were utterly shocked and confused and had stayed indoors so as not to be tainted with the stigma of a visit from the local constabulary. It later transpired that a messenger had called earlier, while James was gardening, to say he was to be detained and on no account allowed to leave until Mr Unwin and the constable came to collect him. The Reverend had been most perplexed and angry. The whole incident would be a bad reflection on his character and the people he employed. He made a mental note to himself to have a stern word with his wife about her choice of maid.

Meanwhile the police wagon jolted its way through the countryside towards Nottingham. James sat in stunned amazement. What exactly was he being accused of? No one had spoken a civil word to him. He was taken to Nottingham jail and thrown into a cell, which was already occupied by two intoxicated women.

Mike Unwin was feeling considerably happier. Things had been getting out of hand and needed to be brought back under his control. While the children and staff were at their work, he had planted one of Joshua Eden's signet rings in James's mattress. He then decided to call a spot search of the premises. By ensuring that James Cooper was absent he felt comfortable that no one would challenge the discovery of the ring. The staff were illiterate fools in his eyes and the children no better. Tom and another male member of staff had searched the boys' dormitory and had found the ring just as he had planned. Mike Unwin then went on to give an award-winning performance of shock, disbelief and sadness as he stood holding aloft the stolen signet ring. So pleased was he with himself that he decided to gather all the children and staff together to preach to them on the evil sin of theft. His 'sermon', for want of a better word, was thankfully interrupted by the arrival of Mr and Mrs Eden, who had been notified as soon as the stolen ring had been discovered.

Leaving the staff to dismiss the children Mike left the workroom with his employers, a warm glow of satisfaction oozing from his person. Once in Mr Eden's study Mike continued with his performance and swiftly brought the Edens up to speed on the situation, boasting of his brilliant skills of detection in finding the culprit. Joshua Eden looked puzzled. Mrs Eden asked if the boy had confessed to where they had hidden the rest of their jewellery. The Master reassured her that he would get to the bottom of this now that the gang leader had been caught. He noted however, that Joshua Eden still wore a look of disbelief. Mike Unwin hoped it was caused by his disappointment in the orphan boys.

'Keep me informed Unwin,' barked his employer. He then turned and left the room, followed by his confused wife.

Returning to the work room The Master was pleased to see all was back to normal. The young children were quietly working, and the staff looked suitably diligent in their supervision of them. He felt the eyes of all present follow his every move around the room as he inspected the work of a number of the children. He questioned the staff as to the efficiency of their work force. This was more like it, he thought. Let them know who the boss is! As he stood by the window admiring the view, he observed two boys in the yard splashing water at one another. Admittedly it was another blisteringly hot day, but it was also a working day. The Master's newfound happiness vanished in an instant. Rushing from the room he grabbed his cane and marched into the yard. On hearing the door open, the boys both scampered to return to their work but one poor lad wasn't quick enough. Grabbing the boy by his collar Mike pushed him roughly to the ground and set about beating him with the cane.

Joshua Eden had indeed looked puzzled and confused. He had not been taken in by the greasy performance of his orphanage manager. He could not believe that children alone could have masterminded such a burglary, obtained the tools to break in with and also break out of an orphanage without help. Something about Unwin's performance did not sit comfortably with him. In the hall outside the study, he had told his wife to return home. He decided to take a look at the dormitory where the signet ring had been found. Unbeknown to Mike he had not been in the carriage as it drove away from the orphanage. Joshua Eden was in fact standing at one of the dormitory windows frowning as he tried to understand how the boys had evaded detection, left the dormitory and made it downstairs and out of the building. Looking down into the yard he could see several boys scraping the earth from the recently picked carrots which they then stacked into a pile of crates. Two of the boys seemed to be in high spirts and after taking a drink from the water trough had begun splashing water at one another, while imitating the theatrical voice of The Master.

'Where are the staff?' muttered Joshua Eden.

Perhaps it was time to have a stern word with Unwin. After all he was paid handsomely to manage the orphanage. Recent events had shown that he was slacking in his duties. At that very moment Mike Unwin strode into the yard. It was clear to see that his blood was up. Little did he know that he was being observed by his employer. Joshua Eden watched with horror as he saw the undernourished child being thrashed to within an inch of his life. He raised his hand and banged it against the windowpane, but it had no effect. Stomping from the room Joshua Eden found his way downstairs and to the back of the building. Throwing open the door he stood red faced and breathless as Mike brought his cane down once more upon the boy's now bleeding back.

'Stop that at once!' he bellowed.

All was silent, Mike Unwin stood hot and flustered, his cane held high ready for the next blow. His arm seemed to have frozen in mid-air and he became uncomfortably conscious of it as he turned to face his employer.

'I caught him…' Mike garbled

'You will leave my employment at once; do you hear me? Immediately!' continued Joshua Eden.

By now the staff member who had been supervising the boys had appeared and stood looking on in amazement. He half expected that he too would be sacked for allowing the boys to get up to mischief.

'Escort this man off my premises and see that he does not set foot on my land again,' ordered Joshua Eden to no one in particular.

Mike Unwin, The Master of Eden Orphanage was gone.

Chapter 15

Unemployed 1860

It took seconds for Mike Unwin to grasp the situation he now found himself in. He was out of work, homeless and worst of all he no longer had his precious jewels! His brain raced, his main concern being how to get back into the orphanage and retrieve the jewellery and cash from their hiding place. He shuddered to think what the consequences might be if someone else discovered his collection. At best they might keep them, but worse would be if that person decided to show the findings to Mr Eden or the nosy jumped up police force. Neither of these possibilities filled him with pleasure. First, he must find somewhere to stay and then make plans to retrieve his gems.

He was angry with himself for his lack of judgement. How many times over the years had he enjoyed the pleasure of thrashing an urchin and had gotten away with it. He had been careless, and this had cost him his job. On the plus side, if he could call it that, James Cooper would soon be convicted as part of the gang that had burgled Eden Manor. Any suspicion regarding his involvement would hopefully vanish. After the trial things would settle down and the four runaway orphan boys might never be found. In his cold heart he dearly wished them all dead. He blamed them for the whole sorry affair. Mike Unwin cared for no one apart from himself, and if justice were served correctly, he got some of what was coming to him at last.

From the roadside he stood looking across at the building which a few moments ago had been his place of employment and home. Once the indignation at being manhandled through the gates had died down, Mike Unwin found himself hiding in a hedgecrow on the opposite side of the road. For the first time in his life he was feeling the emotions of shame and regret. Both cut equally deeply into his cold heart.

The country road was quiet and empty, but Mike could not bear the bright sunlight to shine on him, exposing his disgrace. He had been somebody, he had been respected and feared within the orphanage and in the wider world of Kingminster village. Now he was nothing and, worst of all he didn't even have his nest egg to fall back upon. Sitting on his haunches he waited. He tried to convince himself that all was not lost. If he could speak to Tom or one of the other more malleable staff members he could get back into the building and retrieve his possessions. Once he had those he could move on and start afresh, perhaps in Nottingham Town itself, or even in Derby or Leicester.

At last he heard the clip clop of horses' hooves on the lane. Sinking further back into the hedgerow Mike watched as Joshua Eden's carriage drew up outside the orphanage gates. A footman got down and opened the gates and the carriage passed into the courtyard towards the front of the building. The gates had been left open, no doubt the footman assumed his master would be leaving immediately and had thought to save himself the trouble of closing and opening the gates again in short succession. Without a thought for the consequences Mike ran from his hiding place in the hedgerow, into the grounds of the orphanage. Crouching down behind a large oak tree he scanned the vista for a likely victim. A number of boys and girls were at work in the flowerbeds, weeding and edging the borders. Staff seemed to be conspicuously absent.

'What's the place coming to!' tutted Mike to himself.

Ducking down behind the tree he watched Joshua Eden leave the building and climb into his carriage, which swiftly swept out of the gates. Summoning up his courage and reminding himself that he once ruled in this place, Mike Unwin stepped out from behind the oak and strode up to the front door. Some of the children stopped their work and looked on. His fall from grace was not yet known to all. As he glanced around the children quickly bent their heads to their work, not wanting to risk The Master's displeasure. Ignoring the inquisitive glances from the two staff members, Mike lifted his head high and straightened his shoulders. He then knocked boldly on the front door. The door was opened immediately by Josie, a sour-faced female member of the staff. Mike had always liked Josie, as he felt she shared his repugnance of the orphan children.

'Well I never! We'd been told you're long gone. What you after Mr, eh I mean Mike?' she added as she rattled with laughter.

'I just need to get me bits from me room Josie, then I'll be gone.' Mike smiled his most charming smile.

Josie was not fooled. Although she had once admired his cold hard attitude to their betters, she now saw him for the heartless cruel man he truly was.

'Not allowed to let you in, his Lordship said ta call the police, so you'd best be off.' The door slammed in his face before he could draw breath. 'You ungrateful hag,' shouted Mike to the closed door, and immediately began to rattle the knocker loudly while kicking at the door.

The children and staff in the front garden had now put down their tools and had collectively stepped closer to watch the man they had once feared. This was a show worth watching! The staff felt no compunction to shoo the children back to work. All stood in silence as they watched the once great man bang and kick at the front door, like a child who had been refused a favourite toy. Eventually it was opened by none other than Tom. Josie and a posse of children stood behind him as if ready to attack should Mike attempt to set foot over the threshold.

'You've been told, you're not allowed in the building or anywhere on Eden's land, so go on get lost and good riddance to you!' said Tom, warming to his role. 'We'll do just fine without you, thank you. Now be off.'

The door was firmly shut and Mike once more found himself experiencing that squirming emotion of shame. He wanted to hide now more than ever. The sun seemed to be particularly bright. He had no covering, no tree, bush or hat to hide his bright red face. As he turned and walked towards the open gates a cheer went up from the children and staff, followed by boos and hisses. Keeping his back straight and trying to keep his head held high Mike Unwin once more found himself alone on Kingminster Lane.

Fury and hatred soon replaced the feeling of shame, as he realised he would have to find another way to retrieve his hoard of stolen jewellery. Realising that he would have to bide his time, Mike Unwin turned and headed up the lane in the direction of The Two Bells public house. He would seek shelter there for the night and send word to his Nottingham associates in the morning.

Chapter 16

Millie writes a letter 1860

Back at The Rectory, Millie's emotions had gone from shock to despair and then to fear. On the few occasions that she had been able to keep one of The Reverend's newspapers, she had read the paper from cover to cover. It always struck her that it contained little good news and lots of bad news. Local crime was heard and tried at The Shire Hall in Nottingham, and most usually made the front-page headlines. She felt convinced that James would be tried and convicted without any real evidence. He was poor, had no parents and these two unfortunate circumstances alone would be enough to convict him of a crime he had not committed.

The thought that she could lose her brother and be all alone in the world filled her with dread. How would she cope if she were dismissed from The Rectory? Things were looking bad and she had no idea how she could help her brother. Agnes had never liked having her in The Rectory and had made this plain from the start. She now had even more reason to whisper into The Reverend's ear that Millie came from bad blood and should go. Agnes's usual practice when there were visitors at The Rectory was to hover outside the parlour door to eavesdrop on the conversation. She had been filled with pleasure that day to hear The Rector and his wife discussing the note that she had passed to them from the delivery boy. Millie and James Cooper were bad. At last it looked like they had been found out. Quietly slipping away from the parlour door, she had headed straight for the garden, firstly to make sure that James had not left, but most importantly to listen in on the whispered conversation between the two siblings. Sadly, for her she had heard nothing of any use, just a few names which meant nothing to her.

The remainder of the day passed in a haze of confusion. Agnes took to snapping at Millie's heels and goading her at every opportunity. Millie could do nothing right, and the spiteful range added to her discomfort. Cynthia, being a sensitive soul, had seen how James's arrest had affected Millie, and told her to go to her room and rest. Agnes was beside herself with pique. Rest? What was Madam thinking; she should throw the girl out into the street! But obviously she could say nothing and could only glare at Millie as she headed for their attic bedroom. Upstairs in the room she shared with Agnes, Millie sat on her bed and wept. She cried for her dead parents and cried for her older brother, who had always looked after her and treated her with respect. In the orphanage James had done his best to provide Millie with the odd treat from his work in the fields. Millie had grown thinner by the day. James had been so happy when she had moved into the Rectory to work as a maid. Millie sat on her bed and looked around the room she called home. The small cast iron grate was empty, apart from a smattering of soot which had blown down the chimney. Racking her brain, she tried to think of how she could help James. She needed to find the four runaway boys and pray that someone would believe their story. But something inside her told her that most probably they too would be charged along with James and all would hang, die in jail or be transported.

Reaching under her mattress Millie pulled out a thin makeshift notebook. She had used the odd sheets of paper she had dared to take from The Reverend's desk to make herself a book in which she wrote her ideas and plans for the future. Much of what she had written centred on getting away from the village of Kingminster and returning to Nottingham town. There she and James would set up home. He would work as a barrel maker or 'cooper', as his name suggested, and she would run her own little shop from their front room. Flicking through her book, Millie felt the urge to tear it to shreds. Who was she fooling? Life for people like her was nothing more than an existence. She had watched her beautiful mother drag herself out of bed in the early hours of the morning and walk the three miles into the town centre to work in Joshua Eden's lacemaking factory. Her mother had lost two of her fingers in the machinery at the factory, and despite the difficulty this caused her, she had continued to work a 12-hour day. When she had eventually become too ill to work, she had simply been tossed aside without as much as a thank you from the factory manager.

Sadness seemed to fill the room and wrap itself around Millie like a weighted cloak. She could see no future worth living without her big brother. The stubby pencil she had used to write her notes rolled from between the pages and fell onto the bare pine floorboards. Picking it up Millie threw it into the empty grate, as a fresh wave of tears engulfed her. Eventually when the tears had stopped, she once again thought about how she might be able to help James. Staring at her makeshift book, Millie realised that there was the answer. She had a talent that many girls of her class and generation did not have, she could read and write better than most.

'Write it down and give it to the mistress,' she muttered to herself.

Cynthia was warm and caring, she was all in favour of the

poor achieving a better standard of living than their lot so far. Surely Madam would believe her and speak up for James. Filled with a glimmer of hope Millie retrieved the pencil and began to write. It took several attempts to piece together the events as James had recounted them to her that day in the garden. A few sheets of paper had to be discarded but she felt no guilt at the wastage if it would help to save her brother's life. At last she had finished. Carefully folding the three sheets of paper she placed them in the centre of her notebook and put it back in its hiding place under her mattress. When the opportunity presented itself, she would 'borrow' an envelope from The Reverend's desk and put the letter in it. She had already decided that she would have to wait until Agnes had her afternoon off to show the letter to Madam. She had no intention of letting the prying gossip hear of her plans to save her brother. Agnes would pour cold water on any suggestion and might even tell The Reverend, whom she knew did not like secrets or scandal. Millie felt sure that he would tell her to leave James's fate in the hands of The Lord.

Chapter 17

Doubt 1860

James could hardly believe that he was now in a stinking jail awaiting trial for a crime he hadn't committed. He had been given little information about his crime other than that he was believed to be part of a larger gang of criminals, some of whom had avoided detection by running away from the orphanage. The whole charge and the way in which the case had been handled would have been laughable to James had he been in a position to laugh at the trumped-up charge. He was given no chance to speak up for himself and refute the charge, nor had he anyone to speak for him. He had prayed that Millie might have been allowed to visit him, but so far he had been disappointed. Knowing little of the law, James knew enough to realise that he was to be the scapegoat for the real criminals. He had asked if he could send a message to Mr Eden and had been beaten for his rudeness. There seemed no hope. He prayed that his sentencing would be over quickly and if he were to hang then that too could take place immediately. The poor boy had by now given up any hope of mercy or indeed common sense. Was he really the only one who could not understand how he, a poor orphan boy, could have carried out such an audacious crime without adult help? But clearly the newly formed police constabulary were keen to demonstrate to other would-be criminals that crime would not pay.

Unknown to James, Joshua Eden's voice had been one of the loudest in seeking to find those involved in the burglary at his home. As the days and weeks passed Joshua Eden began to doubt that James Cooper was guilty of any crime other than of being an orphan in his care. Joshua Eden had little knowledge of the circumstances which had led to the two Cooper children being placed in his care, nor had he ever had any reason to speak or acknowledge the siblings. He was aware of the boy's sister. He had heard nothing but good spoken of her by the Reverend and his wife. His own housekeeper had also voiced her doubts as to the guilt of James Cooper, adding that the sister was a gentle, intelligent and hardworking creature, whom she would have happily employed at The Manor if she hadn't already been employed at the Rectory. All this left Joshua Eden feeling decidedly uncomfortable. Someone had to be behind the burglary and that someone was now watching and waiting. There had to be a way to flush him out.

After many sleepless nights he came to a decision; he would send his butler, a man in whom he had total confidence, to attend the trial and speak up for the boy. He hoped that the doubts he had regarding James's guilt would be conveyed to the judge and that the case might be dismissed. He had tried to speak to a prominent magistrate friend, in the hope that James might be released, only to be informed that James was in the criminal system now and as such had to stand trial. If he was innocent then he would be released.

In the meantime, Millie had come up with her own plan to save her brother. She had waited and waited for a suitable opportunity to speak to Cynthia Peabody alone. It had not been easy as her Mistress was often out on social calls or assisting the Reverend with his church duties, as well as teaching at the orphanage. Added to this had been the inconvenience of Cynthia announcing that she intended to take a short break away from Kingminster to visit her parents in Bournemouth. She had not returned home until the weekend preceding the trail. It was now the Friday before the trial. Agnes usually had the Friday afternoon off and on these occasions she would go home to her family on the other side of the village. All through the week Agnes had enjoyed mocking Millie by putting a tea towel around her neck and lolling her head to one side, as if to mimic a hanging. Her snorting laughter had increased Millie's anguish. Each evening, after the Reverend had finished with the newspaper, Millie had scoured it for news of the forthcoming trial. She now knew the date; Tuesday 4th September. Time was running out and she needed to speak to Cynthia urgently. With Agnes out of the house it would be easier for her to pick her moment and catch her Mistress alone. Millie had considered whether she should show her letter to the Reverend and swiftly decided against this. She had never felt comfortable in his presence and apart from Agnes he had been the only one to reprimand her for not paying enough attention to her work.

On the Friday morning Agnes had woken Millie earlier than usual with her coughing and wheezing. For once she was civil to Millie as she begged her to go down to the kitchen and fetch her a glass of water. Millie had at first thought to tell her to get her own water but seeing how ill the girl looked she had taken pity on her. She slipped from her bed and tiptoed down the two flights of stairs to the kitchen. As she made her way back up to their attic room Millie realised that if Agnes was ill she most likely would not be leaving The Rectory to visit her family that afternoon. Millie knew that she would have to speak to The Mistress with Agnes in the house. The letter she had written explaining the events as James had conveyed them to her was safely hidden under her mattress. She had checked its location each evening before going to bed, as she did not trust Agnes, even though she knew that Agnes could not read. Millie had worried that Agnes, being spiteful and cruel, might take her letter and show it to The Reverend Peabody or at worst destroy it.

There was no time to wait for the right moment. James had been gone for nearly three months. Millie knew her only hope was to put her trust in her mistress. She had little faith that Reverend Peabody would act to save her brother. He might decide that the letter was 'nonsense' and put it in the range fire. Mulling this over, Millie decided it had to be today. As she handed Agnes the glass of water she sat on the edge of her own bed and carefully slipped her hand under her thin mattress, feeling for her letter. Agnes was now sitting up in bed having yet another episode of coughing. Millie pulled out the letter and slid it under her pillow. She planned to put it in her apron pocket once she had washed and was prepared for her daily chores. She intended to ask to speak to Cynthia the moment the Reverend was safely out of the house. She would have preferred it if Agnes had been out but she was fast running out of time, and she desperately needed help. She was prepared to allow Cynthia to read her letter and had rehearsed in her head how she would speak to a judge should she be called upon to do so. Millie felt sure that Cynthia would read between the lines and realise that Ned, Robert, George, Herbert and particularly James were not the true culprits. She hoped to persuade her Mistress to speak to Mr Eden who, she believed, had the power to have James released.

Cynthia too had given the plight of James Cooper much thought, and had discussed various outcomes with her husband, before she had left for Bournemouth. Both believed the boy to be innocent but could not understand how he had come by

Joshua Eden's signet ring. If he were innocent who might be trying to frame him? Sadly, the Reverend, mindful of his own situation and a little fearful of Joshua Eden, had told his wife to let the matter drop. They could do no more than they were already doing by giving the boy's sister employment and a roof over her head. This had not been the answer that Cynthia had expected and she had been a little cross with her husband for his dismissal of James. Back in June she had seen how the arrest of the boy had affected his sister. Millie had become withdrawn. She still worked hard but during their visits to the orphanage, Millie had lacked interest or enthusiasm, and was often in tears.

James's trial was now only days away. Cynthia knew that if the boy were to be saved something had to be done soon, but apart from speaking to Joshua Eden herself what else could she do? She had heard that Joshua Eden did not believe James Cooper to be guilty of the break-in at his home, but he was undecided as to James's possible involvement with the missing boys who were now being blamed for the robbery. The police believed they had one of the gang in custody and intended to make an example of him. Of that she was sure. James would probably hang or be transported to Australia as a lesson to all other would-be criminals that the law was tough on theft.

At breakfast it was obvious that Agnes would not be leaving the house that afternoon to walk over to her parents' home on the other side of Kingminster. Throughout the morning she had moaned and snapped at Millie as she struggled with her work.

'Once I'm finished, I'm in me bed,' she kept on saying to no one in particular.

Millie had originally planned to speak to her Mistress after lunch. Agnes and the Reverend would both be out. Knowing that Agnes was staying at home Millie decided to wait until she was upstairs out of the way before approaching Cynthia. No doubt the snooping Agnes would be hovering on the landing listening, but if the parlour door was closed it would be very difficult for anyone to overhear a conversation from two flights up.

The morning seemed to drag. Agnes had not let up on her sniping at Millie and had continued to use every opportunity to put the girl down and find fault with her work. Several times Millie had found it hard not to take the dish cloth and clout Agnes in the face with it as she stood behind her at the sink babbling on about 'low class orphanage scum'! Who did she think she was? Her situation was no different to Millie and James's, apart from her still having living parents. But the stigma of being placed in an orphanage was something that until now Millie had not fully understood.

At last Agnes had finished for the morning and had taken herself off to her bed in their attic room. Knocking gently on the parlour door Millie was greeted by Cynthia's musical voice inviting her to enter.

'Millie my dear what is it?' she asked, seeing the anxious expression on Millie's face.

'It's James Miss. I know he would never steal, and he spoke to Ned just before he was arrested and I've written it all down for you to tell the judge,' blurted Millie, as tears began to run down her face. This was her one chance of saving her brother. All her hopes were pinned on Cynthia believing her tale.

'Slowly, my dear. Take your time, and who is Ned?' asked Cynthia frowning as she tried to take in what Millie was saying.

Millie slowly pulled the letter from her pocket and passed it to Cynthia. After reading it several times to make sure she understood the facts as Millie had stated, Cynthia's expression changed from frowning to excitement. She believed the girl and, even though the letter was not well written and contained many spelling and grammatical errors, it spoke to her heart.

'I knew it!' she cried, and to Millie's surprise she jumped from the sofa and hugged her.

'I will see that this gets to the court, I will take it myself, leave this with me Millie and don't you worry, James will be saved.'

Folding the letter carefully back into the envelope she placed it between the pages of the book she had been reading. Millie took this as a sign that she was dismissed and left the room to return to her chores. As she closed the parlour door, she thought she heard footsteps on the stairs, and guessed that Agnes had been up to her old trick of eavesdropping. Back in the kitchen she felt that a weight had been lifted from her shoulders. She had every faith in her Mistress and knew that she would do her best to free James now she knew the facts.

Chapter 18

A Hidden letter 2019

Lewis breathed a sigh of relief as he closed his bedroom door. Lupin sat down on the bed and Truffle jumped up beside her. Stroking the pup's ears she waited; she tried not to watch Lewis too intently. Something had spooked him, and she wasn't feeling too comfortable herself.

'The brick dust was there on the floor,' Lewis barely whispered.

'I believe you, and if what you're saying is true, no one else has been into the coal house besides you,' added Lupin, by way of reassurance.

'So, who put it there in the first place and then swept it up?' asked Lewis. He was fairly sure he knew the answer.

'Millie!' both children exclaimed at once.

Truffle, thinking this was some sort of game, wagged her tail furiously and jumped off the bed.

'It has to be important and something to do with James. I think she is giving me clues but I don't know why.'

Truffle began to bark and wag her tail as her attention was drawn to something by the fireplace. The puppy was obviously excited and was not in the least bit afraid. Both children turned to look at what had caught Truffle's attention. Visibly there was nothing to be seen, but the atmosphere in the room had changed. By now Lewis knew that they were not alone, and that Millie was also present.

'Millie what is it?' asked Lewis.

Both children jumped and screamed as soot came crashing down from the old chimney filling the grate and spilling onto the carpet.

'The newspaper, I bet that's it,' said Lewis to no one in particular, as he got up from the chair.

Opening the bottom drawer in his chest of drawers, Lewis rummaged until he found the carrier bag containing the old newspaper from 1860. He had decided against showing the paper to his mum until he knew more about its main story, namely the trial of a James Cooper on Tuesday 4th September 1860 at Nottingham's Shire Hall. Mr and Mrs Featherstone had told him that Millie was James's sister, so why was she haunting him?

Laying it flat on his desk, the two children read the account of James Cooper's crime and sentence.

'We learnt about the Victorians and crime as part of our topic on the village,' Lupin said as she scanned the old newspaper for further clues.

'I wasn't that bothered at the time, but I think it was something to do with the Eden family in Victorian times, and how they had been robbed.' she added.

'Your Granddad didn't believe that James Cooper was guilty did he?' asked Lewis. Before Lupin had a chance to answer more soot fell from the chimney.

Millie was definitely trying to tell them something.

Millie was James Cooper's sister, but why was she haunting Lewis and why now? James had been found guilty in September 1860. Surely nothing could be done now to change this or even go back in time and right a wrong in 2019! So why now? And what were the clues leading him to?

'Let's write down what we know and see if we can get a handle on this,' suggested Lupin.

Taking out his notebook Lewis added the following to the notes he had made when he had first found the old newspaper.

Millie and James Cooper brother and sister

Underneath he added:

Both from the spooky orphanage

Taking a pencil Lupin wrote:

Brick dust in coal house?
Old newspaper hidden in the bottom of a wardrobe

That was it, the sum total of their discovery to date. Taking a deep breath and making a quick decision Lewis told Lupin of his dream about the girl who had been crying in the old school room.

'Well that's nowt new, loads of girls cry in school 'cause they don't like it!' laughed Lupin.

Lewis smiled. He was so glad that he had someone to share this with. What might his mother have said if he told her he thought he was being haunted by a Victorian ghost! That aside, they needed to find out what Millie was trying to tell him. So far she had led him to an old newspaper. His internet search had told him that a James Cooper aged 14 had been found guilty of burglary and theft at Eden Manor, in 1860. James had been one of the children living in the ugly Victorian orphanage on Kingminster Lane. The closeness and connection made Lewis feel uneasy. He remembered he had seen the man in the white van acting suspiciously outside the orphanage. But no, he must not let his imagination run riot, the two things could not be linked!

'Perhaps Millie believes James was innocent,' said Lupin. 'Granddad thinks he was set up because he was an orphan.'

Mulling it over Lewis could see how this might have happened in the past. He had watched enough crime dramas, without his parents being aware, to know that before and ever since DNA testing, the police had been known to make mistakes and convict the wrong person.

What's to say that James Cooper had been used as a scapegoat, just because he was an orphan?' suggested Lewis.

'Perhaps that's what Millie is trying to tell you.'

'So how do we find the evidence? He'll be long dead now. It all happened over a hundred and fifty plus years ago?' Lewis sighed.

'Millie is the link and anyway whether it happened a hundred years ago or not his family have been called thieves. How would you feel if your great, great granddad had been accused of something he hadn't done? I bet Millie's life was horrid with people being cruel and calling her brother a thief,' added Lupin, now very much fired up.

'Okay, I get it! So where do we go from here?' asked Lewis.

'I say we listen to Millie, and let her guide us,' said Lupin.

Both jumped as Truffle leapt off the bed and ran over to the closed bedroom door. Turning to look at Lewis she began to whine and scratch at the door. Once the door was opened she behaved as if following someone holding an exciting toy. The puppy ran to the bottom of the stairs leading to the attic and scampered up onto the landing above. Lewis and Lupin followed. Following the puppy, the children entered the room. The puppy was now wildly barking and jumping up at the window, but she was too small to reach the sill. Lewis and Lupin both stood at the window and looked out, but could see nothing of any significance, apart from the coal house door swinging in the wind. But there was no wind and Lewis had closed and locked the door earlier. Perhaps his mum was in there, but he knew this wasn't true. They could both hear her singing in one of the bedrooms below.

'The coal house,' shouted Lewis as he ran from the attic and made for the stairs.

Lupin and Truffle followed. Outside on the patio Lewis took a moment to compose himself and get his breath back. The door continued to swing and bang against the wall as if blown by a gale force wind while the air around it was still dry and hot. Not a leaf stirred on the trees either in the garden or on the patio. The whole scene was decidedly eerie.

Lewis's look of confusion was mirrored in Lupin's face, as both children stepped into the cramped room. The boiler stood silent. Truffle had entered the room first and was now scratching at the wall that connected the coal house to the main building. Lewis reached for the light switch, only to find that the bulb had blown. Leaning forward they struggled to see what had caught the puppy's attention. Lupin was the first to notice the brick dust on the floor. A look passed between them, as Lupin bent forward to feel the wall where the puppy was scratching. This was not just the scent of a mouse that had excited Truffle. She was trying to reach something. For once Lewis had charged his phone and actually had it on him. Taking it out he turned on the torch and shone the light at the point on the wall where Truffle was madly scratching. Lupin pulled the excited pup away from the wall and held her tight by her collar. One of the bricks appeared loose. The dust on the floor must have come from the crumbling mortar mixed with the dust from the old red brick. Lewis knelt down and tried to pull the crumbling brick from the wall, but nothing happened. Truffle continued to yelp, and Lupin found herself struggling to keep hold of the puppy's collar. Once more Lewis tried to dislodge the brick, this time it moved. With the light of the torch Lewis could just about see the corner of what looked like a piece of paper.

'There's something hidden behind here, but I can't get to it,' he told Lupin who was having difficulty restraining Truffle.

The space was cramped and hot. Truffle's excitement had not waned. Lupin stepped out of the coal house and onto the patio pulling the reluctant pup as she went, Lewis followed. Neither child noticed that the door had stopped swinging and now stood wide open and still.

'I think I'll need something to lever it out with,' said Lewis, turning towards the house. Lupin followed dragging the confused puppy. Back in the kitchen Lewis opened a drawer and pulled out a table knife.

'I think this should do it,' he said holding up the knife.

'Truffle is trying to tell us something or show us something in there, but it's not really Truffle is it? It's Millie.' said Lupin.

By now the excited puppy was whining at the back door, desperate to get back outside and into the coal house. Picking her up Lewis gently placed her in her basket in the crate and closed the door. Truffle began to bark and scratch at the crate. She was determined to be involved in the new game whatever that might be.

'We'll leave her here until we can get at whatever it is that's hidden under the brick,' said Lewis.

'What's going on and why are you so dirty?'

Both children jumped as if they had seen a ghost as Lewis's mother appeared in the kitchen doorway. Looking down at his clothes Lewis noticed the brick dust and also the soot. His hands and nails were covered in both. In contrast Lupin looked her usual pristine self, with not a hair out of place and not a speck of dirt on her person.

'Truffle ran in to the coal house and I had to get her out,' mumbled Lewis lamely.

'Keep the dog under control Lewis, she's still a puppy, she

needs to have boundaries,' snapped his mother, as she turned and headed back upstairs.

'Blimey that was close!' laughed Lewis. Lupin grinned as she looked at the knife Lewis was still holding at his side.

'Good job she didn't spot the knife, otherwise you would have been for it,' said Lupin. 'Come on, let's try and find out what's hidden out there.'

Once again they stepped into the coal house, Lewis turned on the torch on his phone and looked for the spot on the wall where Truffle had been scratching. In the dim light he was unsure where to look. Lupin had now taken out her mobile phone and had also turned on the torch.

'Here it is,'

'Good, hold the light steady and I'll try and see if I can move the brick.'

Kneeling, Lewis used the knife to scrape away the crumbling mortar. He eased out the loose brick. Clinging to the underside was a yellowing envelope. By now Lupin was also kneeling.

'This has got to be another sign from Millie,' said Lewis.

Neither said a word. Each was engrossed in digesting the events that had taken place so far. Millie was clearly trying to lead Lewis to something and was leaving them clues and signs. The envelope was most unquestionably old. Stepping out of the coal house door and dusting off their clothes, both felt a tingling sensation surge through their bodies. Millie was real, or at least a real-life ghost; if a ghost could be 'real life'! That was the gist of the unspoken words that passed between the two young people.

Chapter 19

Lewis and Lupin Read Millie's letter 2019

There was little time to do anything other than stuff the envelope into his pocket. Mum had reappeared to inform Lupin that her parents had been trying to get hold of her, she was to return home immediately. A look passed between them. Lupin left, knowing full well that she would return later that evening to read the contents of the envelope with Lewis.

After a stern dressing down from his mum, Lewis eventually went up to his room. Carefully taking the envelope from his pocket he put it with the old newspaper in the carrier bag and once again hid the bag in the bottom drawer of his chest of drawers. He ached to tear it open and read its contents, but he knew that he would have to wait until Lupin's return that evening. They were in this together. She seemed to understand him and had not scoffed or laughed at his suggestion that the house was haunted.

It was growing dark and Lewis was beginning to despair that Lupin wouldn't return. The sound of a car pulling up outside the house made him push his mobile phone into his pocket. He had been composing a text to ask if she would be coming back. Opening the front door Lewis watched as she walked towards the gate. She was grinning from ear-to-ear. Someone, in the car, was calling to her, but she seemed not to be listening.

'10 o'clock, do you hear me?' called the man in the car.

'Yes, Dad, I promise I will be ready by then,' answered Lupin, without so much as a backwards glance.

Truffle now appeared at the front door, excited at the return of a familiar face. After a few minutes fussing the puppy, and a polite word with Mrs Henry, the three of them climbed the stairs to Lewis's bedroom. Closing the door, Lewis opened his wardrobe and reached up to the shelf. Taking down several items of clothes he threw them onto the floor behind the closed door. Seeing the quizzical look on Lupin's face, he whispered that it was to stop his mum from coming into the room. The clothes would act as a form of door stop, which would give them enough time to hide anything they did not want her to see.

Truffle, thinking this was yet another new game, promptly started to chew at the sleeve of Lewis's favourite hoodie.

'Stop it, leave it!' Lewis shouted as he tried to get the puppy to let go of the top.

Eventually Truffle relented and instead lay down on the pile of clothes and began to investigate each item with her nose.

Clearing a space on the computer table Lewis retrieved the carrier bag containing the old newspaper and letter. Carefully he opened the envelope and placed the folded sheets of paper it contained on the desk. Millie's letter written in broken and misspelt English told how George, Ned, Herbert and Robert had run away from the orphanage. It went on to explain how George had found the pouch containing the ruby and diamond pendant and matching earrings. The last sentence made both children sniff and wipe tears from their eyes as they felt her anguish. Over and over again she had repeated that James was innocent and had done nothing wrong.

'That's it,' said Lupin, 'James was fitted up and so far we have no idea what happened to him. I suspect he would have been hung,' she added.

Lewis found it hard to speak. He was choked up with emotion, a lump had blocked his throat making it hard for him to swallow.

'Poor Millie and James, they wouldn't have stood a chance. Do you think we could search some more and see if we can find out what did happen to him?' said Lewis, staring at the girl's plea to save her only living relative.

'It won't be easy. We're talking about stuff that happened over 150 years ago,' added Lupin.

'Your grandparents have lived here all their lives and know lots about the village. I say we start with them and find out what else they know. You say James Cooper was mentioned in your topic on Victorian local history. There must be more information we can find,' said Lewis, as ideas whirred around in his head.

'If he was innocent as Millie says, we could try and find out who was guilty, then again perhaps not,' he added as he realised the enormity of what he was proposing.

'I say we let Millie tell us what to ...'

At that moment Truffle began scratching furiously at the wardrobe door. With her paw she managed to claw open the door. Lewis remembered the old newspaper he had found hidden under the wardrobe's false bottom. The atmosphere in the room was charged with electricity. Taking out the newspaper the children read again the account of James's trial.

'I think you're right Lewis, we should start by asking my Gran and Grandpa,' said Lupin as she re-read the newspaper account from September 1860.

Before leaving Lewis's bedroom, the children took another look at their list of facts about the case of James Cooper. They typed the names mentioned in the letter but were unable to find anything on the children who had inhabited the orphanage in 1860. They decided that they would share some of the facts they had with Lupin's grandparents but would not on any account mention Millie. If they were questioned too closely by anyone, they would simply say they had gleaned their information from the internet. As Lewis made to switch off his computer a flash of light caught his eye at one of the upstairs windows in the old orphanage.

'I thought that place was empty,' he observed pointing at the building.

'It is, no one's been round for ages. Gran and Granddad have a set of keys, and usually get a phone call to let them know when someone is likely to want to get into the grounds or building. Apart from the other day there's been no one near the place,' replied Lupin also looking at what looked like the light from a moving torch in one of the upper rooms.

'I'll phone Gran now,' she added as she fished her mobile phone out of her pocket.

After a short conversation Lupin looked decidedly confused. She explained to Lewis that no one had been scheduled to visit the building, and that her Granddad had thought he had heard someone in the grounds when he had been working in his rose garden. He had dismissed the notion and had thought perhaps it might have been a cat. Both children stood and stared at the orphanage. Someone was in there and using a torch. The ground floor windows had all been boarded up, possibly to prevent anyone breaking in, but the upstairs windows had been left intact as no one would have been able to break in through one of these without considerable difficulty. So who and why was someone in the building?

'I know you're going to think I'm mad, but do you think the orphanage is haunted too?' asked Lewis.

'It's possible, but let's face it, are we talking about a Victorian ghost with a torch!' laughed Lupin.

Lewis laughed too, but still the glint of torch light continued to move from window to window. Both children were suddenly brought to their senses by a sharp ripping sound as Truffle tore the sleeve from Lewis's favourite hoodie and held it up for their inspection as if she had just caught a live animal.

'What now!' screamed Lewis in frustration, and the puppy wagged her tail even more enthusiastically as Lewis tried to retrieve his torn sleeve.

'Lewis what's the matter?' called his mum as she tried to push open the bedroom door. Truffle began to bark and held onto the torn sleeve and jumped onto the bed.

'It's okay Mum, Truffle is playing we'll be down in a bit.'

'What's happened to the door?' asked mum.

Scooping up the clothes and hastily throwing them into the wardrobe Lewis pulled open the bedroom door. Lupin stood at the window and Truffle lay on the bed pulling at the cuff of the torn sleeve.

Mum took one look at the scene and did something Lewis had never seem her do before. She shrugged her shoulders and quietly closed the door as she left the room.

'What!' exclaimed Lewis. 'She's definitely losing it, I was expecting a full-blown lecture!'

'Be grateful, my Mum would have roasted me if I had let the dog on the bed, let alone let it tear up my clothes,' replied Lupin as she continued to stare at the old orphanage.

Lewis could see that she was disturbed by the torch light.

'Why would anyone be in there at this time? What are they looking for? I don't like it, something just doesn't feel right, and my Gran and Gramps are living right next door. Do you think they'll be alright?' muttered Lupin.

Chapter 20

Agnes and Millie 1860

After her conversation with Cynthia, Millie had relaxed and put her faith in her Mistress. That evening Agnes had questioned her about what she had been doing in the parlour. Millie had simply looked beyond her and told her to keep her beak out of her business. This had infuriated Agnes who had been enjoying watching Millie slide further and further into despair. What could have happened to give her such a lift? Agnes had tried to listen in on the conversation in the parlour but, short of climbing down the stairs and standing outside the door, she had been unable to hear anything of any use, apart from Cynthia's cry of excitement. She longed to tell the Rector that Millie was up to something but knew she would be on thin ice if she had no evidence. She might even be dismissed for eavesdropping on his wife. Millie Cooper was bad, rotten and scheming, just like her brother, but no one could see it apart from her! Agnes was beside herself with jealousy. Well she would watch her and the Mistress more closely, maybe she would find out what they were up to.

Cynthia had given considerable thought to her conversation with Millie and had re-read the letter several times. She was in a dilemma. Should she show the letter to her husband? What might be his reaction? He had on several occasions reprimanded her for being far too lax with the servants and had not taken to Millie at all. Since the whole episode of James's arrest at his home he had hinted on several occasions that perhaps it might be better for Millie to return to the orphanage. Cynthia felt a little sad that as a man of God her husband cared so much for his own reputation. In her heart she knew that she would not show him the letter or speak to him of the conversation she had had with Millie. However, Joshua Eden or even his wife might listen. But she had her doubts on that score too. When all was taken into consideration it might be best to act alone. She would organise her day for a shopping trip into Nottingham on the coming Tuesday and attend the court and present Millie's evidence as well as speaking up for James. The more she thought about it, the better the idea seemed.

The weekend seemed to pass far too slowly for Millie. She was on tenterhooks every time someone rang the doorbell. Agnes's cold seemed to be taking its toll on her ability to work, and Millie found herself doing the work of two people. But despite this her spirits were high. The Mistress would free James and all would be well!

The morning of Tuesday 4th September began warm and cloudless. As Millie washed and dressed, her head felt light with excitement. Today the truth would be told, and James would be free. Going about her morning chores Millie hastened to take her Mistress her morning tray. She had passed the Reverend in the hall on his way to performing the last rights for a dying man in the neighbouring village of West Leake.

'My wife appears to be unwell. Take care of her, some beef tea might help,' announced the Reverend as he left the house.

Unwell! Millie could not believe it. Perhaps it was part of Cynthia's plan not to involve her husband. Millie's heart began to race. Agnes appeared at her side, and seeing her agitation took full advantage of the situation to goad Millie about the trial.

'He'll hang as sure as my name is Agnes May Grimes,' she stated as she blocked Millie's path.

There was no time for Millie to reply. Quickly pouring the boiling water onto the tea leaves and checking that she had set the tray correctly Millie picked it up and headed upstairs to her Mistress's bedroom. Cynthia lay in the bed looking flushed and hot. With Millie's help she was able to sit up, but it was clear that she would be unable to make the eight-mile journey into Nottingham for the trial.

'Millie, my dear I'm so sorry, my head is swimming and I feel as though I might be sick!' she gasped. 'I don't know what to do about poor James.'

'Perhaps I could go, if you told the gardener to take me in his trap,' Millie suggested.

'That won't be possible. He's taken his annual holiday. I don't think you would be allowed in the court and certainly not to speak up for James.' Cynthia added. 'We will just have to hope that the judge is sensible and sees that James couldn't have committed the burglary by himself.'

'But that's the problem,' Millie almost screamed. 'They think he was part of a gang, that's what the papers say! He'll be convicted and hanged,' she added as she burst into tears.

'Don't worry, Agnes can take the letter up to the Manor House and give it to Mr Eden. I believe he plans to attend the trial.'

The thought of Agnes taking her letter anywhere was abhorrent to Millie.

'I'll take it Madam, I can run up to the Manor now,' Millie said as she stretched out her hand for her Mistress to pass her the letter.

Time was running out; Millie desperately needed her letter to reach the judge before the trial began.

'It's in my book on the table in the parlour,' Cynthia added as Millie raced from the room and collided with the ever-present Agnes who just happened to be passing the master bedroom!

For a fleeting moment Millie saw recognition flash across Agnes's face. Silently and moving quickly Agnes fairly tiptoed down the stairs and into the parlour, closing the door behind her. Millie almost jumped the flight of stairs and flung open the parlour door. Agnes stood panting in the centre of the room, but something about the triumphant grin on her flushed face told Millie she was too late. Agnes had her letter. The book that had contained the letter lay open on the occasional table together with Cynthia's sewing box and embroidery. Pushing Agnes aside Millie picked up the book and shook it – nothing!

'He'll hang,' snorted Agnes triumphantly and stepped out of the room.

Disbelief, frustration and an urge to kill coursed through Millie's body. What was she to do now? She could go back upstairs and tell their Mistress, but she knew that Agnes would deny taking her letter. Shaking the book again and praying that she had misjudged Agnes, she found nothing. In desperation she began to pull the books from the shelf and shake each one hoping that her letter had been misplaced. In her heart she knew she would find nothing. Tears of frustration ran down her face as she left the room and turned to make her way up the stairs to her Mistress. In the hall her path was blocked by the smirking Agnes.

'Looking for something?' she whispered.

'You won't get away with it, I'll tell the Mistress what you've done, and you'll be sacked.' Millie hissed back. 'Now get out of my way.'

Pushing Agnes aside she ran up the stairs. Knocking on the bedroom door Millie entered to find her Mistress bent over her washstand. She had just been sick. After clearing up the mess, and helping Cynthia back into bed, Millie tried to explain that the letter was no longer in the book and that she thought that Agnes might have it. Cynthia struggled to grasp what Millie was trying to say, and once more had to be assisted to the washstand into which she retched violently. She eventually collapsed on the bed and turning her back to Millie told her she was too ill to deal with Agnes now.

'It's in my book, I saw it yesterday evening. Surely Agnes wouldn't dream of taking something that doesn't belong to her. She's been with me for years.'

So that was that, Millie was dismissed. What could be done? Agnes had her letter, her only hope of freeing James. Millie wanted to rip out her vile tongue, but she knew that would serve no purpose other than to confirm to all that mocked her for being poor that she and her brother were the worst kind of people. Trying to calm herself, she decided to try to reason with Agnes. If she could just get her letter back, she still had time to run up to the Manor House and give it to Mr Eden before he left for Nottingham.

Chapter 21

Spite 1860

Agnes could feel her heart pumping against her rib cage as if it was trying to thump its way out of her body. She had the envelope secure in her bodice and was prepared to turn out her pockets if her Mistress asked her to do so. Both girls stood facing one another in the hallway. Millie had great difficulty in not rushing at Agnes and tearing out the rats tails she called hair!

'Give me my letter,' Millie demanded.

'What letter?' sneered Agnes.

'The Mistress is ill, otherwise I would get her now,' said Millie trying another tack. 'She told me where she had left it and I'm to take it up to the Manor, so give it to me now!'

Agnes smirked even more and drew herself up to her full height.

'What letter?' she asked again as she replaced the smirk with a screeching laugh, neither of which enhanced her pinched features.

'You know what I'm talking about, so hand it over, otherwise I will go upstairs and tell The Mistress that you have stolen from her.'

Just for a fleeting moment a look of doubt crossed Agnes's face, but only for a moment. The grin was back, as she made a great show of turning out her pockets.

'What letter?' she laughed, and with a flourish she turned on her heels and strode towards the kitchen.

Millie was deflated. What could she do? Time was running out. The Mistress was sick, and Agnes had her letter! In desperation she ran after Agnes, grabbed her by the arm and pulled her into the scullery. Kicking the door shut, she set about beating and scratching at her in an uncontrollable rage. She was so angry and intent on beating the truth out of the girl that she didn't hear the door open and the Reverend Peabody enter the room. In an instant he had pulled the screaming Millie from Agnes, who lay on the floor curled up into a ball as her only means of defence.

'Clean yourself up girl and get out of my sight. My wife is ill, and I come home to find you fighting! I knew we shouldn't have taken you in!'

'She's mad Sir, I done nowt wrong, she just set about me,' added Agnes now crying and looking very forlorn.

Reverend Peabody wasn't interested in listening to Agnes. The sight of his two servants fighting had unnerved him. Violence was abhorrent to him and to have it in his own home, well that really was the limit!

Upstairs Cynthia had heard the commotion but had been unable to get out of bed and make her way downstairs. She had heard her husband's raised voice and lay in her bed waiting for him to come up and explain what was happening below.

On entering the bedroom, Reverend Peabody was greeted by the sight of Cynthia leaning over the washstand bowl as she yet again attempted to empty the contents of her stomach!

'My dear, whatever is the matter?' he asked trying to avert his eyes from the bowl.

'Archibald, I think that you're going to be a father,'

'Good Lord, my darling, oh my! Shall I send for a doctor?'

'I don't think so. Mother warned me that this might happen,

and that it wasn't anything to worry about. But Archibald, what was that commotion I heard downstairs?'

'Oh, eh, oh yes, I found the orphan girl attacking Agnes, I'm sorry to say it but I do not think we should keep that girl, she is far too hot headed.'

Lying back on the pillow, Cynthia tried to focus on her husband's face. He looked cross and confused. He had never taken to Millie. Cynthia knew he hated the scandal that now surrounded her regarding her brother. But Cynthia had made a promise to Millie and she intended to honour it.

'I think James Cooper is innocent. Millie has evidence to that effect. She wrote a letter which I said I would take to the trial. I distinctly remember leaving it in my book, I saw it there last evening. I told Millie to ask Agnes to take it up to Joshua Eden, as I believe he intends to attend the trial today. Millie says the letter is no longer in the book, so have you by chance moved it my dear?'

'Letter? Moved it? Never! I don't understand. Are you sure you don't need a doctor?'

'Archibald, I am fine. Now will you please help me up and I will try and get to the bottom of this.'

Cynthia made as if to stand but fell back onto the bed as her head reeled.

'You're going nowhere darling. Lie back down and I will get Agnes to bring you up some beef tea.'

Another wave of nausea swept over Cynthia, making it impossible for her to even speak. Lying back on her pillow she prayed that the dizziness and sickness would soon pass.

Millie knew that Agnes had her letter and had probably thrown it into the range fire by now. What was she to do? She was frantic; time was running out, and she needed to ensure that Ned's evidence reached the court, otherwise James would hang. Millie felt sure that if a judge heard Ned's account of that night in June there would be enough doubt regarding James's involvement. Without the letter James had no defence. Fully recovered from Millie's onslaught Agnes strode into the scullery, grinning from ear to ear.

'Tick tock, tick tock, them that's thieved will be hung,' she sang as she danced out of the room and set about continuing with her preparation for the mid-day meal.

'Please Agnes, I'm begging you, give me my letter, it's no use to you as you can't even read, so just let me have it back,' pleaded Millie.

'Me Dad always said to be watchful of them that think they're better than everyone else, and you an orphan brat at that! What letter you on about?'

Millie was unable to reply, as Reverend Peabody had appeared in the doorway, to tell Millie she was needed upstairs. As she passed Archibald Peabody Millie paused for a moment and considered pleading her case to him; the look of disgust on his face as she passed was enough to silence her. She would receive no help from that quarter. Upstairs Millie had no time to think of James as Cynthia was struggling to sit up in the bed and seemed to be running a temperature.

'You're very hot Madam, shall I run and fetch the doctor?'

'I think you had better, this is not how mother said it would be!'

Glad to escape the house and thinking that she might just run up to the Manor House and try her luck there, Millie quickly removed her apron, washed her face and tried to tidy her unruly curls. As she slipped out of the back door, she wondered whether she could make Eden Manor her first port of call, but she had seen how unwell her mistress had been, and felt duty bound to attend to her needs first. By the time she had run up Kingminster

Lane to Dr Lamb's house, she could barely breathe. Speaking quickly to his housekeeper she left immediately. Crossing the road she turned left onto the Gotham Road and was very nearly knocked down by a passing horse and rider.

'Watch where you're going girl, you startled my horse!' shouted the angry horseman. Barely glancing at the man, Millie kept her head low and muttered her apologies. She then asked the horseman if he knew if Mr Eden was still at home.

'He is indeed at home, but I very much doubt that you will be able to have an audience with him,' chuckled the rider, as he settled himself more comfortably on his horse and turned to take a closer look at the servant girl who was asking after his master.

'Goodness me you're the Cooper girl! I recognise you from the Summer Ball when you and your young friend …Agnes, that's it, Agnes helped out with the extra guests. Now what might you want Mr Eden for?'

Allowing herself to look closely at the horse rider, Millie recognised Joshua Eden's butler, Mr Carlton, a kindly and warm-hearted man. Just for a moment she considered telling him her dilemma, but decided against it, after all what could he do?

'I urgently need to pass a message to Mr Eden. I have to hurry there is no time…'

And with that she ran once more towards the back entrance of Eden Manor. Reaching the door Millie took a moment to organise her thoughts. She straightened her skirt and brushed her hand through her hair. Her curls had broken loose from her customary bun and were hanging limp on her perspiring face.

'No time,' she muttered to herself, and with a quick glance at her boots she knocked hard on the large oak door.

She could hear voices coming from within, but she had a

long wait before someone eventually answered the door. Every second that ticked by brought James closer to the hangman's noose. Why was everyone moving so slowly today of all days? After what seemed hours she was led into the kitchen by a surly kitchen maid. There had been a garbled conversation with the kitchen maid, who seemed unable to understand a word spoken by Millie. The cook grasped the situation immediately and understood the fear and desperation which was written as if in red ink across Millie's face.

'Sit down child, you have nothing to worry about. Mr Eden has sent Mr Carlton to Nottingham to attend on his behalf at The Shire Hall, you have nothing to fear. Mr Eden believes your brother to be innocent, as do we all,' said the cook.

Millie could hardly believe what she was hearing. James would be freed. She had some difficulty in understanding what this might mean for herself as well as James.

'I saw Mr Carlton just now, so is it true he will free James?' muttered Millie.

'That's what he said as he left not a minute ago. "That young man's been wronged, and Mr Eden wishes to put it right." Those were his exact words if I'm not mistaken.' said cook as she glanced around the steaming kitchen for affirmation.

Several heads nodded in agreement, and a few of the servants stepped forward curious to see the face of the girl whose brother was be saved from the noose. As the words were spoken Millie found herself unable to breathe. She made as if to stand, reaching out for the kindly woman but at that moment, whether from relief or stress, she fainted on to the kitchen floor, hitting her head on the corner of the large scrubbed pine worktable.

Chapter 22

Truffle's Discovery 2019

In one area Lewis and Lupin had made a significant break-through. It appeared that The Master of the orphanage at the time of James's trial had originally lived in the village. He had been known to many as a thoroughly unpleasant and vile man. Lupin's granddad had heard from his father, her great, great grandfather that Mike Unwin had a younger sister who had also lived in the village. She had worked at The Two Bells public house. She had frequently bemoaned her lot in life, explaining to all who would listen about how she and her brother had been cheated out of their inheritance by Joshua Eden. It was generally known in the village that Mike Unwin had been sacked by Joshua Eden shortly after James's arrest. Stories as to the exact reason for the sacking had circulated regarding theft, murder and even torture.

What was of particular interest to Lewis and Lupin was the closure of the orphanage in the December of the following year. The remaining children had all been moved to a nearby workhouse in Southwell. Granddad Featherstone had told the children that as a boy he had often heard the men in the village talking about the theft of untold valuables from Eden Manor none of which had ever been recovered. It had been suggested that Mike Unwin was involved in some way and that was why

Joshua Eden had sacked him. Village gossip then and now was that Mike Unwin had known where Joshua Eden's gems were hidden.

The children considered what they had heard and decided their best course of action was to write to the present-day Eden family, and ask if they could shed some light on the dismissal of Mike Unwin in June 1860. Also, why the orphanage had closed so suddenly. Lewis and Lupin were interested in the story of the theft. Theft that had resulted in James Cooper's arrest and trial. One place connected the three parties and that was the orphanage. James had been convicted of theft, but no jewels were ever recovered, Mike Unwin had been dismissed at around the same time as James's arrest, and a year later Joshua Eden had closed the orphanage.

A letter was eventually written and posted to the current Eden family, the contents of which explained how Lewis and Lupin were researching the history of the village from its Victorian past to the present day. They wanted to learn more about the disused orphanage, the Old Rectory and Joshua Eden, the man who had built the orphanage. After much arguing they decided that they would not mention the burglary that had taken place in 1860 nor mention James Cooper's name. They would wait and see what sort of response they received from the family. In essence it was what had happened to James that was their main interest, but they feared that bringing it up too soon might cause the family to dismiss any enquiry they might make about the orphanage.

The summer holidays passed only too quickly, and it was soon September and the start of a new school year. Lewis was due to start school at the nearby comprehensive school in East Leake, where Lupin was already a pupil. They had spent the remainder of the summer trying to find out what had happened to James. His fate could have been one of three options, namely hanging, reform school or transportation. As to what had happened to George, Ned, Robert and Herbert, they were none the wiser. Without full names and more information, their searches had thrown up nothing on the four boys.

Mrs Eden had replied to their letter and had given them some valuable information. They had already learnt from a visit to The National Justice Museum in Nottingham that James would most probably have been sent to Western Australia, if he had been transported. Otherwise to a Reformatory school in Surrey. Neither Lewis nor Lupin liked to think of the third option, that he might have been hanged and was now lying in an unmarked grave. Mrs Eden's letter explained that Mike Unwin had been dismissed, but the reason for this she had no idea. She did however, allude to Joshua Eden keeping diaries, and said she would to try find them and look at what he was writing about in 1860.

What was most interesting was her explanation for the closure of the orphanage. Apparently, her husband's great great grandfather had doubted that James and the other boys were the real perpetrators of the burglary at Eden Manor. He had been sad that his well-meaning plan to provide homes for orphaned children had resulted in one of them being convicted of burglary and theft from his own home. He had lost the heart to continue with his venture to improve the welfare of the local poor but had still continued to provide employment for those who wanted it in his lace factory in Nottingham. The orphanage had closed in December 1861 and had remained closed until its sale to Addbridge Construction in 2017.

Millie had not appeared to Lewis in any form for some time. Finding her letter in the coal house seemed to be the last of her clues. Sitting on his bed on the first day of term, Lewis read again the letter they had received from Mrs Eden. He felt a wave of sadness wash over him as he thought about James Cooper. The boy had become as real to him as any living person. He cared deeply for his sad and unfortunate life. The Victorian Joshua Eden had been a good man and must also have felt deeply hurt that his good intentions had ended in theft from his own home. Fired up with indignation, Lewis decided that they must try to clear James's name. First, he had to find out exactly what happened to James after his trial. Kissing his mum and Truffle, Lewis set off to walk the short distance to the bus stop on Kingminster Lane outside The Two Bells pub. One comfort he took from this lull in their quest to find the truth regarding James Cooper, was that this first week at school would be a short one. Today was Thursday, only two days before the weekend, when he and Lupin could continue with their search.

The first day at the new school had gone well for Lewis. On the bus home Lewis and Lupin made plans to meet up that evening once they had eaten their evening meal and completed their homework. They would take the dogs for a walk and plan another way in which they might be able to find evidence that would clear James's name, and find out what happened to him when he left the court on 4th September 1860. Having Truffle was brilliant for Lewis; his mum was pleased to see his enthusiasm for taking the young pup out for regular walks. Lupin would usually go across to her grandparents and take Goldie, Truffle's mum, along for the walk.

Both children had fallen into a familiar route for their walk and contemplation; this consisted of meeting up outside the orphanage gates and from there they walked down Kingminster Lane, turned left into Church Lane, past Lewis's home and the church and into Eden Park. Strictly speaking this wasn't a park at all, but an extension of the Eden's back garden. It consisted of several fields that had once grown corn and wheat during the

Victorian Era. The fields linked up with the back entrance to the abandoned orphanage. An overgrown tree-lined track led from the back gates of the orphanage half a mile up to Eden Manor House. They had often imagined Joshua Eden in his carriage making the short journey from his home to the orphanage. It was likewise easy to imagine James walking through the gates into the open fields to start his work each morning. There was a melancholy sadness about the scene, as both children looked at the boarded-up ground floor windows of the abandoned orphanage and tried to imagine what life might have been like for Millie and James.

Lewis had tried to imagine life without his parents, and the thought of losing both had filled him with dread. He felt a deep sadness for the siblings and was determined to solve the mystery and at the very least clear James's name. For now there was no way of knowing what had happened to the boy. One thing he did know was that Millie had had no contact with James after his arrest. She would have little knowledge of what had happened to him after his trial. Perhaps that was why she seemed so hell bent on proving his innocence. Lewis, Lupin and Truffle, were now her tools in unearthing the truth. Well, he would do all in his power to help the ghost girl.

They had reached the fields and the two dogs were now free to chase about in the open fields. Both ran to and fro only stopping to sniff the ground from time to time on the trail of a rabbit, squirrel or pheasant. Lewis and Lupin discussed their next move in trying to find descendants of James and Millie Cooper. They had drawn a blank at each turn so far. Millie's silence had worried them both. Having guided them so far, she seemed unable to give them any further clues. Lewis had hardly dreamt of her or felt her presence in the house.

It was a cool September evening and the sun was just

beginning to set in the sky. Truffle and Goldie had run backwards and forwards chasing a ball, then a bird and lastly two excitable pheasants. Goldie lay on the grass panting at Lupin's feet, but Truffle had run off towards the far field in the direction of a number of derelict barns and the stream.

Having called her several times and getting no response, Lewis set off in the direction of the barns. He hastened his step when he heard an echoing bark from what sounded like the inside of one of the buildings. The children had been warned on several occasions that the barns were unsafe and that they should not enter them, or indeed let the dogs anywhere near them. Lewis knew from the sound of the bark that Truffle had somehow entered one of the barns and had found something that had excited her. Her bark was becoming louder and more urgent; he feared she had perhaps hurt herself or got trapped in some way. Lupin also understood the urgency of the puppy's barking and had quickly clipped the lead back on Goldie and run in the direction of the noise.

Both Lewis and Lupin reached the larger of the barns at the same time. The entrance was sealed and bolted so Truffle must have found another way into the building. As they circled the barn, they saw where the puppy had entered the building. A wooden side door had rotted away in the bottom left hand corner leaving a convenient hole for an animal or even a small person to crawl through into the barn. Lewis knelt down and called to his puppy. Her response was an even louder series of yelps, Truffle sounded in distress! Pushing himself through the gap he entered the dark and smelly barn. The interior was heavy with dust and age-old dirt. Dust motes drifted down to the floor and then circled back up again towards the roof space. Reaching for his phone he turned on the torch and shone it around the large empty space. Over in the far corner Lewis was horrified to see Truffle struggling and pulling at something that was caught around her front paws.

'I can see her. She's got herself caught up in some rope or something,' shouted Lewis to Lupin.

Lewis made his way across the dirt strewn floor, towards the yelping puppy. In the dim light he could vaguely make out something shiny and bright that had attached itself to the dog's paws. It wasn't a rope but looked more like a necklace attached to strands of thread and sacking. As he drew closer Lewis found that he was struggling to breathe. Something about what had ensnared the dog made his heart race. Truffle was caught up in what had once been a fabric bag. Its contents appeared to be a long string of diamonds intertwined with red stones which looked like rubies. Lewis calmed the puppy and tried to unravel the mess that had caught around her paws. This was not easy as the puppy was so distressed; she struggled and pulled away each time he tried to hold her still to release her from the tangled strands. He soon realised why she had been yelping. One of the stones, which looked like a ruby, had cut into her paw. A thin trickle of blood was oozing from between her claws.

'Lupin, can you help me please. She's hurt her paw and is caught up in something which you need to see,' he shouted over his shoulder.

Lupin looked around for somewhere to tie Goldie but could see nothing apart from the barn itself. Pulling the dog to the main door she hastily wrapped and tied the lead around the padlock and hoped that Goldie would not pull herself free. Rushing back to the side door she crawled into the barn. It took several seconds for her eyes to adjust to the light and to spot the torch light in the far corner. Turning on her own phone, she too used the torch app to make her way over to where Lewis and Truffle were still struggling in the corner. Between them they eventually managed to calm the puppy enough for Lewis to carefully untangle her from the strands of cotton thread and the necklace. Neither child could believe what they were looking at. It had to be the diamond and ruby necklace that had been part of the items stolen from Eden Manor in 1860!

'You know what this is don't you?' whispered Lupin. 'But what's it doing in here?'

'Look over there!' exclaimed Lewis as he pointed his phone into the far corner where a pile of broken stones lay next to an old birds' nest. In the torch light they could see the glint of diamonds sparkling on the dirty floor. Lewis held Truffle close while Lupin carefully threaded her way over to the glittering object. It was the most tasteless and ostentatious earring. Shining her torch around the area she soon spotted its twin.

'These, these... I don't believe it! Do you think Millie knew?' stammered Lupin.

The enormity of what they had just uncovered was not lost on either of the children. They had spent many days over the summer discussing the robbery that had led to James Cooper's arrest and trial. Both had seen a copy of the painting in which the Victorian Mrs Eden had been immortalised wearing the items they now held in their hands. Truffle continued to whimper. Goldie, who obviously felt she was missing out on the excitement began to whine and scratch at the barn door in an attempt to free herself. Without a word, Lewis and Lupin quickly searched the surrounding floor area and picked up the threadbare cotton pouch. They were unable to put the necklace and earrings back into the pouch, as the fabric had almost disintegrated. Scraping off the twigs from the birds' nest, they stared at the threadbare pouch. All that was holding it together were a few thin strands of thread and the original drawstring.

Pocketing the jewels and the pouch, both carefully crawled out of the barn pulling the reluctant puppy between them. The bleeding had stopped and apart from licking her wound Truffle appeared to be unharmed. Releasing Goldie from her restraint the children sat down on the damp grass to take another look at their find.

'What do we do now?' asked Lupin.

'These have to be the ones stolen back in 1860. Remember Millie's letter, she said Ned had said they had found them outside the orphanage window,' said Lewis, as he inspected the heavy necklace and its matching earrings.

'So how did they end up in the old barn?' Lupin asked more to herself than as a question to Lewis. 'I think the boys must have hidden them in the barn. Probably in the birds' nest that was on the floor next to the jewels. They must have hoped that they would have been found by one of Mr Eden's farming staff. Either way I believe Millie's letter, and think that George, Ned, Herbert and Robert had nothing to do with the robbery. But who was it and where are the rest of the jewels that were stolen at the same time?'

'I think we go back to my house and see if Millie will appear and give us a clue as to what our next move should be,' suggested Lewis.

Gathering up the two restless dogs the children walked slowly back down the overgrown track to The Old Rectory. It was getting dark by this time. Lupin was anxious to go home, as she had noted two missed calls from her mother while they had been in the derelict barn.

After a brief call to her mother, Lupin informed Lewis that she had to return home immediately. Her mother had told her in no uncertain terms that it was a school night and she needed to be indoors before it got dark. Both were met at Lewis's door by Lewis's mum, who insisted that she drive Lupin home and return Goldie to the Featherstone's house. An unspoken agreement passed between Lewis and Lupin which was to hide the jewels and discuss it tomorrow.

Once upstairs in his bedroom, Lewis tentatively took another look at the necklace and matching earrings. His instinct told him that these items were extremely valuable and were probably worth a small fortune. Placing them and the tatty cotton pouch in the carrier bag which contained the newspaper and letter, he pushed them into the back of his wardrobe. He felt uncomfortable having the jewels in his possession. Several times that evening he considered showing them to his mother and asking her advice on what to do next. But he knew what he needed to do next. They had to take them to the police, along with the newspaper and Millie's letter. But something about this decision didn't fill him with confidence. Would James's name be cleared? Also, where were the rest of the stolen items? Would anyone believe that he had been visited by a ghost from the past who had helped them find the items? To these and many more questions Lewis felt that the answers would all be negative. It was imperative that he and Lupin first solve the case and then told all. How they would do that seemed impossible to imagine. One thing that was certain was that the jewels would have to be returned to the Eden family, sooner rather than later. But for now he would simply sleep on the matter and discuss their next move tomorrow. With these and many more thoughts running through his head Lewis fell into a troubled sleep.

He woke suddenly in the early hours of the morning with his heart racing. For the first time in weeks Lewis had dreamt of the orphanage. In his dream he saw Millie, standing in the shadows, watching a tall hard-faced man wearing a frock coat.

The man was reprimanding a group of young children, barking orders at them as if they were animals in need of taming. Millie slunk into the shadows and followed the man, who appeared to be unaware of her presence. She trailed him to a small room on the ground floor at the back of the orphanage. Taking a key from his pocket and turning to check that he had not been followed, the man unlocked the door and entered the room. He shut and locked the door behind him, and there the dream ended.

What was she trying to tell him now? She must know that he and Lupin had found the diamond necklace and matching earrings, so was she now giving him another clue to follow? Lewis felt sure Millie's appearance in his dream had been no coincidence. Lying in his bed Lewis thought over the events of the previous evening. The orphanage was the link, and the man? Lewis felt pretty certain that the stony-faced man had to be The Master, Mike Unwin, the man who had lost his job shortly after the arrest of James. So what was his part in this mystery?

Quietly getting out of bed, Lewis opened his bedroom curtains. In the dim moon light he could barely make out the dark outline of the old orphanage. That building held the clues to solving the mystery.

Chapter 23

The fate of Mike Unwin 1860

Reeling with indignation and hatred after his dismissal, Mike Unwin made his way to The Two Bells public house. It had always been a favourite haunt of his. Now it would also have to be his home. His sister Jane was in attendance behind the bar, where she worked as a barmaid. Jane Unwin was every bit as vile as her elder brother. Working in the bar had given her many an opportunity to extort money from some of the public house's more colourful regulars. On hearing the news of Mike's dismissal, she had plied him with gin, in the guise of consolation. Jane hoped he might just let slip where he kept his hidden fortune, which he often referred to as his "nest egg". It was a topic he loved to talk of when under the influence of alcohol. Unfortunately for Jane, he had never divulged where this nest egg lay, only that it was sizable. Enough to keep him in comfort for the rest of his life.

Jane knew that her life as a barmaid would inevitably come to an end. Her options were few; try to marry well, which was highly unlikely in her case, or make enough money from the regulars who had loose tongues. This option had so far not been enough to keep her in good clothes and regular meals. For now, she had a room to live in over the pub. It was not ideal, but she knew she was luckier than most. She had never liked the town and the work in Joshua Eden's lace factory. When Mike had become Master at the newly opened orphanage, she had decided to follow him back to the village of Kingminster. Jane was acutely aware that she could not continue to live over the public house for ever. Soon her looks would fade, and with these her chance of a good catch in the husband stakes. Not that she held out much hope on this score in Kingminster. Her brother had always seemed to be the answer to her prayers of a life away from the smell of stale gin and urine.

'What did you do then?' she asked, on seeing the sour face of her brother enter the public house in the middle of the day.

'I've been thrown out, no time to pack, just shoved out like old baggage.' whined Mike.

'All me stuff, still in me room, nowt but the clothes I'm stood in,' he added, seeing the knowing look on his sister's face.

'You must have done something. Eden likes you, he wouldn't just chuck you out,' replied Jane.

'So, I thrashed one of the lazy idiots, and he saw me. That was it! Expect he was none too happy at having his fancy house robbed.'

'I heard about that, is it true some of them orphans did it?' she asked, keen to hear the gossip first-hand.

'Don't know owt about the robbery, but I wouldn't put it past that lot to have done it,' he added with relish.

He was now thinking. Plant the seed and watch it grow. Jane liked to gossip, and he would give her plenty to ensure he was never implicated in the recent robbery. Just for a second, and only a second did he consider telling her the truth. At times he longed to share his plans for the future with her. For no other reason, than to boast to her of the success he had made of his life, in comparison to hers. But he swiftly remembered that she too was an Unwin. Unwins trusted no one, not even family. He needed to keep his wits about him and let nothing slip.

'Give us a gin and let me think for a minute,' he snapped, as he headed for the snug.

'Oh, and I need a bed for the night,' he called over his shoulder.

Mike sat in the desolate pub and sipped his drink. He had to find a way back into the orphanage to retrieve his hidden gems. He considered each member of staff in turn and abandoned asking any of them for help. Perhaps Jane could go and ask to collect his possessions? Definitely not! She would probably disappear once she had his nest egg. There had to be another way. Charlie and the others who had willingly stolen for him - now there was a possibility. He thought long and hard how he could get close enough to any of his boys to ask for their help.

Abandoning this idea, Mike sat and nursed his drink. Tomorrow he would make a call on his Nottingham associates. Perhaps, it might be time to let them know that there was more stuff hidden away in the orphanage. They could break in and collect it for him. A shudder passed down his spine. He knew the moment he told the Nottingham set that he had retained certain items for himself, they would gladly retrieve them and that would be the end of it. Thieves could not be trusted! He would sleep on it. Tom and the other staff might think they had got the better of him, but he would have his revenge. For now he must keep his own counsel.

Chapter 24

James's Trial 1860

On the morning of James's appearance at Nottingham Shire Hall, a mixed crowd had gathered on the pavement outside, some eager to see "justice" done, and some calling for clemency for the young orphan boy. *The Nottingham Journal* had diligently reported the case from the time of the break-in at Eden Manor, to James's subsequent arrest. Speculation was rife; many believed the boy to be innocent and that he was being used to divert the blame away from the true perpetrators. But who these were none but themselves knew.

Several times Mike Unwin's name had come up in the conversations in the tea shops, public houses and private homes of both the rich and poor. His dismissal made many question his possible involvement in the robbery. However, on the night of the robbery he had a cast iron alibi. So did James Cooper, but no one seemed to care about this. He was an orphan, poor, young and defenceless. Crime had to be punished and the police had at last caught their man, or so they believed.

Mr Carlton, Joshua Eden's long standing and trusted butler had been given strict instructions by his employer to attend the trial. His instructions were to listen to the evidence given against the boy, and to take note of who had attended to watch the proceedings. Joshua Eden was by now convinced that there was more to the recent spate of burglaries than just a few orphan boys. He suspected that some of those involved might attend the trial to see James convicted. Mr Carlton had grown up in Kingminster village and knew the local faces, both good and bad. As the village was some eight miles from Nottingham town Mr Carlton did not expect to see any of the local workers or indeed criminals. He had wondered why his Master had stressed the point of checking who attended the trial. But he was not paid to think for his employer, so he had mounted the horse and set off to make the journey to The Shire Hall in Nottingham.

His chance meeting with the boy's frantic sister had pressed upon him the urgency of his task. Mr Eden had expressed serious doubts as to the guilt of James Cooper. The boy had been arrested and was now in the hands of the legal system. Joshua Eden could hardly ask for the boy to be released without concrete evidence, and this he did not have. All he had was a feeling that the boy was being used as a scapegoat, and that others more cunning and older were involved. Joshua Eden had a kind heart and cared for those around him. This care for others was particularly evident in his relationship with his butler. On many an occasion in the past he had confided in Carlton and trusted the man's judgement. If ever a person needed someone to confide in now this was most definitely the time. The two men had discussed the robbery at Eden Manor and the other local robberies from the prominent houses in the surrounding area. Both felt that all was not the work of a few orphan boys. There had to be someone or several persons orchestrating the robberies and disposing of the stolen items. After much deliberation it was decided that Carlton was to attend the trial and speak up for the boy. He knew most of the children in the orphanage either by name or sight and had occasionally spoken to James when he and others had brought fresh provisions up to the Manor House. His mission was to have the boy released and to have him brought back to Kingminster to Mr Eden's care.

The road to Nottingham was little more than a dirt track winding a route through the villages of Gotham and Clifton. A shorter route could be taken by riding across country through the fields which had now been harvested and lay dusty and barren. Wishing to save himself some time, Mr Carlton decided that he could cut his journey time by half if he took the shorter route. Setting off at a gallop, he found himself enjoying his ride on the beautiful chestnut mare. Unfortunately, as he rode out of Gotham the horse suddenly reared up and made as if to throw him. He struggled to calm the animal and safely dismount. Mr Carlton tried several times to settle the horse, but his efforts were in vain. As he walked, holding onto the bridle, he noticed that the horse had begun to drag its front right hoof.

It took several minutes of soothing words for the animal to eventually calm down enough for him to take a look at the hoof. The horse had thrown a shoe. Mr Carlton remembered that there was a blacksmith in the next village of Clifton. Looking around he realised that by going off the road he was now in the middle of a dusty field. There was not a house or person in sight. His choice was simple; continue on foot to Clifton or to turn back and seek out the blacksmith in Gotham. Gently coaxing the horse he managed to lead it to a nearby copse and tether it to a tree. Heading back towards the road he hoped to hail a passing cart and reduce the time it would take him to walk to the village of Clifton. Sadly, on this day there was no one in sight.

Taking out his watch he checked the time. He realised he was now running late. The trial was due to start in just under two hours. He had to move quickly otherwise he might not make it to Nottingham in time. Hurrying across the field he cursed his misfortune under his breath. He had been enjoying the view from the height of the chestnut mare and had not paid attention to where he was going. He wondered what Mr Eden would have to say when he received the bill from the blacksmith. The journey across the parched dry fields was difficult and extremely dusty. Uncollected stems of wheat, forgotten in the fields, combined with the baked dry clay soil made it difficult for him to keep his footing.

Twice he had turned his ankle. He was now hot, sweaty and dirty. His customary crisp white cotton handkerchief had become a crusty rag, from its much use at wiping the sweat from his brow and the dirt off his hands. At last he sighted the village of Clifton. Picking up his pace, he hurried in the direction of the blacksmith's forge. Fortunately for Mr Carlton, he was well known in the village and was on first name terms with the blacksmith. After explaining his predicament, he was soon mounted on one of the blacksmith's own horses, and once again continued on his journey to Nottingham. He had been reassured several times that Mr Eden's mare would be collected, re-shod and ready for him to collect on his return journey.

Sticking to the road for fear of another mishap Mr Carlton finally crossed the bridge over the river Trent and reached the town of Nottingham. He had never visited The Shire Hall, but Mr Eden had told him to head in the direction of his lace factory and from there ask for directions. On this day there was no need for him to seek directions, as he turned into the Lace Quarter he spotted a large crowd gathered on the pavement in front of an impressive building. Many were shouting for justice for the poor. He made his way through the crowd to the back of the building and dismounted from his horse, which he tied to a post. People were spilling out onto the pavement and several boys in high spirits had begun to throw rotten vegetables at the well-dressed folk leaving the building. Something must have happened to make the crowd so angry. A stirring in his stomach told him that it might have something to do with the Cooper boy. Glancing at his watch he realised he was late and most probably had missed James's trial. His heart began to beat faster, urging him forwards. On the steps of the Shire Hall, he observed a well-dressed group of people deep in conversation. Making his way across to them he asked where he might find the judge who would be hearing the James Cooper case.

'It's over. I'm afraid you're too late,' answered one of the men, and turned back to continue his conversation with the assembled group.

'Excuse me for once again disturbing you, but I most urgently need to speak to the judge who is responsible for the trial of James Cooper,' he exclaimed.

'You had better have a word with one of the clerks, there's one over there,' said the man and pointedly turned his back on Mr Carlton, signalling that the conversation was over.

Looking in the direction of the man's pointed finger, Mr Carlton spied a clerk in the doorway, and hurried over to speak to the man. It took several attempts and several interruptions from the clerk for Mr Carlton to finally grasp that James had been tried. He had been found guilty of burglary and robbery. Mr Carlton was now in an uncontrollable rage. He demanded that the clerk take him to the judge immediately, but was told that this would not be possible, the judge was in court hearing other cases. Trying a different tack, he asked if he might be taken down to the cells to speak to the boy. Once again the answer was negative. He was horrified to hear that James had left the building along with other condemned men bound for goodness knows where. There was nothing the poor man could do but curse his own misfortune that morning and trust that his

Master might be able to intervene once he was made aware of the facts. He sincerely hoped that James could still be saved, but knew that once a sentence was passed the law could not easily be changed.

With his head bent low he left the building and retrieving his horse made the journey back to Clifton to exchange horses.

On hearing of James's fate, Joshua Eden immediately dispatched a letter to The Shire Hall explaining his doubts as to the guilt of the orphan boy.

That night sleep did not come easily to several of the inhabitants of Kingminster village. Mr Carlton felt regret and shame for not making it to the court on time, he felt that he had failed both his Master and the boy.

News of the trial and its consequence had also reached The Rectory and Orphanage. Millie had fainted at the news that she would never see her brother again. Even the spiteful Agnes had experienced a stirring in her stomach akin to guilt at her deliberate hampering of Millie's efforts to have her brother released. Archibald and Cynthia had suggested that they all attend the church that evening and pray for James Cooper. Agnes, who still had Millie's letter tucked inside her bodice made the decision not to destroy it. She decided that she could still redeem herself with her employers by producing it at a later date if need be. She could pretend that Millie had not searched in the right place. Taking the letter she entered the coal house and looked around for a place to hide it. She felt she could not take the risk of hiding it in the house, and no one would dream of looking for anything other than coal in such a dirty and unwelcoming place!

The next morning the mood in The Rectory could only be described as sombre. Archibald and Cynthia were quietly rejoicing in their good fortune at the prospect of becoming parents, but both were acutely aware of Millie's dismay and low spirits. Cynthia, much to her husband's annoyance, had gone up to the attic bedroom to comfort the distraught girl. Her kind words and reassurances did nothing to calm Millie.

In Millie's mind everyone had failed James including herself. She was now all alone in the world, her loving brother gone. She had no information as to the nature of his sentence. He might well be dead or lying in a jail awaiting transportation. She had hardly slept and had spent the night trying devise a way in which she could help James, if he were still alive. So far her best solution was to find George, Ned, Herbert and Robert. They could tell their tale of how they had found the jewellery pouch and confirm that James had nothing to do with the robbery or indeed any in the past. Alive or dead Millie was determined to clear James's name.

Finding the boys would be difficult. It was now some three months since they had run away from the orphanage. They could be anywhere! Perhaps if she could speak to Joshua Eden himself he might help with her search for the four boys? Questions, questions and more questions and all seemed to lead to a dead end! Even the word 'dead' had made her shiver. If James was alive there was still time to save him.

'Millie my dear, is there anything I can do to help? I'm so sorry I was unable to attend the trial yesterday,' whispered Cynthia, as she stroked Millie's forehead.

'I would like to speak to Mr Eden. I know it's not done for the likes of me to speak to someone so grand, but I need to tell him what I know. My letter was my only chance of saving James and I know Agnes took it. But I need to tell Mr Eden the truth, so the real thieves can be caught, and James freed if he hasn't already been hung.' sobbed Millie.

It was the same story again. Cynthia felt sad that she too

had failed the brother and sister. She decided that perhaps the girl's outlandish request might be best dealt with by Mrs Eden. Leaving Millie pale and sobbing into her pillow Cynthia left the attic room and prepared to make a morning call on the Eden family.

In the carriage on the short journey to Eden Manor Cynthia rehearsed her speech. The Edens were good people and fair, but she was a little afraid of what she would be asking of them, or rather telling them what needed to be done in order to free the Cooper boy, if he was still alive. At Eden Manor she stood momentarily in the hall admiring the family portrait of Joshua with his wife and two daughters. Poor Clarissa, what had become of her? The artist had captured their likenesses accurately and the rubies and diamonds Mrs Eden was wearing seemed to glitter in the daylight. Mr Carlton, the butler, appeared and escorted her into the morning room where the Edens both greeted her with offers of tea and cakes. After much civility and polite niceties Cynthia was finally able to explain the reason for her unusual visit. Joshua Eden was visibly hurt and dismayed when he heard Millie's account of that fateful night in June.

'I thought as much, but evidence is what we need to bring the real perpetrators to justice.'

'But what's to be done about James Cooper?' asked Cynthia. Her only concern was to save James.

'I'm afraid we can do nothing. He has been tried and convicted, the law cannot be changed, I had hoped that Carlton might have secured his release, but sadly he arrived too late,' explained Joshua Eden.

After a lengthy discussion on crime and punishment Cynthia was glad to take her leave of the family. Once home she was informed by Agnes that Millie had not left her bed. Agnes had cried crocodile tears as she told Cynthia that Millie had threatened to kill her if she came anywhere near her that day. It was all getting too much for Cynthia who was once more feeling nauseous. In the attic bedroom Cynthia did her best to recount Mr Eden's words as accurately as she could but could see from Millie's face that she was totally without hope.

'I can do no more Millie.' said Cynthia with a heavy heart. 'You rest today, and I will come and see you later.'

And with that Cynthia got up from the bed and went downstairs in search of something to settle her churning stomach.

Joshua Eden was also at a loss as to how he might help the boy. He had been right when he told Cynthia that nothing more could be done. He silently prayed that James was still alive. He could be freed if enough evidence was found to convict the true perpetrators. The next day *The Nottingham Journal* carried a front-page piece recounting the trial of James Cooper and others.

Chapter 25

Publicity or Not? 2019

On the Friday morning Lewis woke feeling thick headed and tired. He had lain awake for what seemed like hours trying to put the pieces of the puzzle together. Today he knew they would have to show the jewels to his mother and she in turn would no doubt take them to the police. Lewis felt a proprietorial need to hold onto them a little longer. He was anxious to tell their version of the events that had led up to them finding the jewels. At the bus stop, Lewis pulled Lupin to one side and quickly told her of his dream the previous night. Both agreed that after school they would ask Lupin's parents to be present when they showed their findings to Lewis's mum. This would include the letter, the old newspaper, the torn cotton pouch, and more importantly, the jewellery. On the school bus in whispered tones they agreed that they would not mention Millie or indeed the orphanage. Both children felt that the police and their parents would find it hard to give credit to a ghost girl from 1860.

The day at school seemed to drag and neither child learnt very much at all. At lunch time they both took their packed lunches to a quiet corner of the canteen and discussed what they needed to do next. Would Millie continue to appear, or had she done what she needed to do so far? It was agreed that the puzzle was far from solved. Lupin was curious about the man in the frock coat. Both felt confident that he had to be Mike Unwin, but as to his part in the mystery the children were none the wiser.

Internet searches during the summer holidays had yielded nothing on Mike Unwin, or indeed any of the staff working at the orphanage back in 1860. Combined with Millie's silence the children had almost given up trying to solve the mystery of James's false accusation of robbery. Finding the ruby and diamond pendant set had brought Millie back into Lewis's life. Both agreed that the dream was significant and important in solving the mystery. The clues they had been given were The Master and the orphanage. Somewhere within its walls they would find more clues possibly about Mike Unwin, James and the four boys who had run away from the orphanage, but what they were looking for neither child knew.

'I imagine Mr and Mrs Eden will be over the moon to recover their ancestor's jewels,' mused Lupin, as she stirred her yoghurt pot.

'Hopefully, they might believe that James Cooper was innocent of the robbery,' added Lewis.

'We'll soon know, won't we!' said Lupin as she decided to discard her half-eaten lunch. There was no time for further conversation, as the bell rang, and the canteen was cleared in preparation for the afternoon lessons.

That evening on their customary dog walk, Lewis and Lupin came to the decision that they would have to go into the deserted orphanage and look for further clues. They agreed that they would hang on to the ruby and diamond pendant set until they had had time to sneak into the orphanage and see if they could find anything to prove that James was innocent. Lupin recalled that when her grandparents had been asked to be key holders for the orphanage, the manager of Addbridge

Construction had asked if Mr Featherstone would like to take a look inside the building. Her granddad had jumped at the chance and had come back with tales of the old building, describing the dormitories and work rooms, surprised to find that a lot of the old fixtures and fittings were still in place in the building, including the iron cot beds.

'Do you remember in the summer seeing a light in the upstairs rooms of the orphanage?' asked Lupin.

'Now you mention it, in my first week in Kingminster I saw a man acting suspiciously outside the gates, but I thought he might have worked there,' added Lewis, thoughtfully. Pieces of another puzzle were beginning to slot into place in his head.

'Your Granddad said he'd heard noises coming from the building, but when he'd contacted the developer they said no one had been round,' continued Lewis. 'Do you think someone might be hiding or even living in the building?'

'Oh no! I hope not. We had better keep a watch on the place and see if anything strange is happening. I don't fancy going into such a large old building if someone might be camped out in there,' said Lupin with a shudder.

Both children were silent for several minutes while the dogs ran backwards and forwards looking for something to chase as it was clear no one was going to throw the ball for them. It was finally agreed that as Lewis had a good view of the building from his bedroom window, he would look out for signs of movement inside the building. While Lupin's parents had no problem with her spending a great deal of time with her grandparents, she knew they would be suspicious if she asked to sleep at her grandparents' house during term time. As they walked back up the lane both stopped to look through the gates of the orphanage. All was silent.

Once home Lewis racked his brain for a better hiding place

for the pendant and earrings. He didn't want his mother to find them and ask lots of awkward questions before he and Lupin were ready to take them to the police. Walking from room to room in his shabby Victorian Rectory, Lewis thought about the hiding places that Millie had used. Climbing the stairs to the attic bedroom, Lewis took one last look at the magnificent if somewhat ostentatious jewellery. Putting them and the cotton pouch, or at least what was left of it, into another carrier bag, he then carefully sealed it with tape and pushed it into the small chimney cavity.

'Millie keep this safe, we will clear James's name,' he whispered to the empty room.

Feeling satisfied that his hiding place was secure, he went downstairs to his bedroom. Somewhere in amongst his possessions he had a pair of binoculars, a gift from an uncle who had noticed his fascination with birds. After much searching, he finally found them and turned them towards the orphanage. He now had an almost perfect view of the right side of the building and the large wrought iron gates. All was as it should be. No lights and no sign of the white van parked in the lane.

Chapter 26

Freedom 1860

Ned returned to the desolate barn with a heavy heart. He had been glad of the opportunity to explain to James, of all people that they had stolen nothing. By talking through the events of that night he was able to put them into some sort of order in his jumbled mind. He knew in his young heart that he and the other runaway boys were no longer simply four boys who had made a bid for freedom. Everything had changed the moment George had stumbled upon the cotton pouch. They would be hunted as criminals. Thieves who had stolen from the one person who had given them a home, shelter and security. Ned had always felt a warmth towards the Eden family.

Nothing could be done to turn the clock back now. Salt tears ran like rain down his dirt smeared cheeks. George, Robert and Herbert had gone. Perhaps he too should leave. No doubt a search party would be out looking for them. To stay so close to the scene of the crime was madness, he must move on and soon. He wondered where the others had gone. George had promised he would leave the pouch somewhere where it could be found and returned to Mrs Eden. Ned wondered where that place might be. He mused that the contents of the pouch would have kept all four of them in luxury for the rest of their lives, if they had been mindful to keep the jewels. But theft was not something any of them had ever considered.

Curling into a small ball, Ned hugged himself as the tears continued to flow uncontrollably. He eventually fell asleep, and dreamt of his mother. In his dream she held him tight and rocked him gently in her arms, as she stroked his hot sweaty brow. It was dark when he woke to find himself still curled in a tight ball lying on the hard barn floor. There was no sign of the others. At that precise moment Ned knew that he was totally alone in the world. At the tender age of 10 Ned had had little experience of the world at large. Where to go, and how to get there without being caught, was now his main concern. George had often talked of Derby when they had worked together. George's family had moved from the Derbyshire countryside to Nottingham in search of work. Perhaps he could aim for Derby and hide out there?

In the early hours of the morning following the robbery, Herbert and Robert had said a hasty goodbye, explaining to George and Ned their reasons for leaving so soon. They were afraid to be too close to the orphanage. The barn had only featured in their plans as a place to lie low over night and from there to move on. The chance finding of Mrs Eden's precious jewels had frightened each of the boys in different ways. All knew the consequences if they were caught. As close friends, Herbert and Robert decided to stay together and make their way towards London, hopefully without detection. Further than that they had no other plans. It had been a tearful parting as each of the boys had said a final farewell. None had asked George where he intended to leave the pouch.

Ned had seemed unable to grasp the danger they were all in. He had suggested to George that he would try to speak to one of the boys from the orphanage who would be working in the field that day. He seemed unable and unwilling to leave the safety of the barn, and the familiarity of the landscape he knew so well. George had tried to talk him out of this dangerous idea, explaining that if he were seen and caught he would be beaten if not hung. But Ned had been adamant. He needed to tell someone the truth, and who better than a fellow orphan. Understanding that Ned had made his mind up, George considered his own plans. He had finally decided upon a suitable place to leave Mrs Eden's jewels. He then planned to make his way back to Derby. It was after all the town of his birth. Other than that he remembered nothing of the place. But he had to go somewhere, and as far away from Kingminster as possible. Once there he would find someone who could write and send a letter to the Eden family, explaining where to find Mrs Eden's necklace and earrings. The pendant and earrings had lain heavily upon him in more ways than one on that first night of freedom. He knew that they had to be returned. George prayed as he left the barn that the pouch would remain safely hidden until he was far enough away.

Chapter 27

Lewis goes to London 2019

Once again sleep did not come easily to Lewis. He lay in his bed running through the events so far and felt sure that the man he had seen hanging around outside the orphanage in the first week in Kingminster was significant. Addbridge Construction had sent no one to the building all summer but on at least two occasions noises had been heard and a light had been seen in the upstairs rooms. Maybe Lupin was right and someone, a tramp or vagrant, was living in the empty building. If that was the case, he doubted that he would feel comfortable about going into the supposedly deserted building.

Eventually Lewis fell into a deep sleep, only to wake early before sunrise. Opening the curtains he reached for the binoculars which he had left on his laptop. All was quiet, perhaps they were imagining it and no one was living or hiding out in the building. The man in the white van might have been taking a call or was simply lost. The noises Lupin's granddad had heard might have been the old pipes rattling. They certainly rattled a lot in The Old Rectory! Satisfied with his explanation Lewis washed and went downstairs to prepare breakfast for himself and his mum.

It was Saturday, and there was no chance for any further detection. Lewis was being picked up by his dad and was to spend the weekend in London. On any other day he would have been delighted at a weekend back home with his old school friends. However, his eagerness to solve the mystery of the deserted orphanage was uppermost in his mind, which made him resent the time he would waste while away. He would have preferred to have stayed in Kingminster with Truffle and Lupin, piecing together the the puzzle. He felt confident that if his mum were to tidy his room she would find nothing out of the ordinary. The ruby and diamond pendant and matching earrings were safely hidden in the attic chimney. He knew his mum respected his privacy, and would never look in his drawers or wardrobe. She had rarely set foot in the attic rooms, and he very much doubted that she would choose to do so this weekend.

The weekend in London passed extremely slowly for Lewis. He enjoyed his time with his father, but nothing made him wish he still lived in London. In the short space of six weeks, he had grown passionately fond of his new home and the village of Kingminster. He was keen to get back to the village and make further plans for solving the mystery of the Eden Manor burglary and other robberies in 1860. He was determined to have James Cooper's name cleared of the charges of burglary and theft.

On the Sunday evening, once Lewis had returned home, he asked if he could take Truffle round to Lupin's house. His mother was a little put out at the suggestion. She had spent the weekend alone, apart from the pining dog. She grudgingly agreed to his suggestion and drove him and Truffle over to the Andersons' home on the other side of the village. After going around and around the puzzle several times the children decided that the only way they would solve the mystery was to look inside the orphanage. Both agreed that it needed to happen sooner rather than later. Monday evening after school seemed as good a time as any. If they found nothing to help them in their quest to prove

James's innocence, they would show the jewels to their parents and ask them to inform the police. While not feeling particularly happy with this plan, both knew that they could not hold on to the jewels much longer. Too many questions would be asked about why they hadn't handed them in earlier.

At home in bed that night Lewis dreamt of Millie once again, but his dream was cut short by the agitated sound of Truffle barking. Both mother and son were alarmed at the noise and wondered if someone had been trying to break into the house. Armed with Lewis's cricket bat they both tentatively crept down the stairs. The security lights had come on outside, but there was no sign of a break-in.

'It must have been a fox,' said mum without conviction. Lewis could see that she was visibly shaken.

Releasing Truffle from her crate, mum stood at the back door with the cricket bat. After a short sniff around the garden, the puppy returned and once more settled down in her crate. Upstairs in his room Lewis decided to take one last look at the orphanage before trying to sleep. Picking up his binoculars and turning off his bedroom light he looked towards the dark looming shape of the building. There was no need for binoculars! Across the field in the black of night he could see the silhouette of the orphanage. Two lights similar to someone moving by torch light could be seen on the first and second floor. At least two people were in the building, and by the movement of the torch light they had to be looking for something.

Lewis's heart raced, what could he do? Surely Addbridge Construction would not have sent workers to the building at this hour! This had to be someone either looking for something or as Lupin had suggested, sleeping rough in the building. Lewis felt sure that a tramp would not be moving from room to room, and using a torch at three o'clock in the morning. This had to be at least two people searching for something.

Mum had gone back to bed, and he didn't feel that waking her would be to his advantage. Reaching for his mobile phone, he noted that the battery was nearly flat. He sent a quick message to Lupin telling her what he had just seen. Climbing back into bed he glanced at the silent phone on the bedside table and considered getting back up and plugging it in to charge. Tired and worried Lewis decided the phone could wait until the morning. There would be plenty of time for it to charge while he washed, breakfasted and walked Truffle.

Millie's appearance in Lewis's dream was nothing unusual. But this time when Lewis woke up he felt that he had actually experienced the dream first hand. Millie had taken him inside the orphanage, so real was the impression of the dream. The smells, the sounds and the people had all been real. He had walked with Millie through what must have been the laundry. They had then stood side-by-side as they watched a group of young girls scrubbing greying sheets by hand, their pinched faces registering no emotion, as their red raw hands worked automatically.

The man in the frock coat was shouting orders at the woman who was supervising the girls. Millie and Lewis stood side by side surveying the scene. They then followed the man into the kitchen and out into the yard. Everyone he encountered stepped aside or looked away, for fear of catching his eye.

'Mr Unwin sir, Mr Eden is in the study and is asking for you,' said a young man as he bowed his head to the frock-coated man.

So, this was the great Mike Unwin! Hunching her shoulders Millie seemed to glide away from The Master taking Lewis with her. He found himself alone in his dream, standing by a water pump and trough, in what must have been the back yard of the orphanage. A gate was swinging on its hinges, and somewhere a bell was ringing. The sound was familiar.

'Why have you set your alarm for such a ridiculous time?' Lewis's mum stood at the side of the bed with a frown fixed firmly on her face. He knew that look only too well.

Lewis struggled out of his bed and reached for his mobile phone. Lupin had replied to his text from last night.

'Talk on the bus,' it read.

Plugging his mobile phone into the charger Lewis wandered into the bathroom. There was no time for breakfast. He needed to take Truffle for a quick walk and then hurry up the lane to the bus stop. Ridiculously early hour! She had no idea how much he had to do before leaving for school! He decided to take Truffle up Kingminster Lane past the orphanage and the Featherstones' cottage. This would give him a chance to take a closer look at the building and see if there were any signs of someone in the grounds or building.

At the gates to the orphanage he stopped and looked. He could see no signs of any disturbance, apart from the familiar half circle in the gravel, where one of the gates had been pushed open. All looked normal, but as he scanned the upstairs windows Lewis had the distinct feeling that he was being watched, but from which of the many windows he was unsure. Perhaps it was just his imagination running wild, after the torch light of the night before. There was no time for contemplation. Turning he ran back home with Truffle happily trotting at his side. Kissing his Mum and rubbing Truffle behind the ears Lewis left for school. By the time he reached the bus stop he was just in time to catch the school bus. Lupin was standing in the doorway of the stationary bus pleading with the irate bus driver to wait for Lewis, while the driver was shouting that if she didn't move he would close the door on her!

Lupin listened without interruption as Lewis recounted

the events of the previous night. Neither child could find an explanation for Truffle's unusual behaviour. The torchlight in the orphanage was a mystery and not a little worrying. Both felt uneasy about entering the derelict building, particularly if it were occupied.

Chapter 28

A New Career 1860

Mike had stayed on at The Two Bells public house for the remainder of the week. James Cooper was now awaiting trial. So far no one had hinted that he Mike Unwin, was to blame in any shape or form for the robbery at Eden Manor. Somehow, he doubled that he would have heard any such rumours. The locals were in awe of him. His diminished status had not changed the way he was viewed in the village. No one would dare to voice any of their suspicions within earshot. However, Jane who listened to every bit of gossip in the village, would have told him if she had heard any disparaging remarks concerning him. It had always been her way to taunt and belittle him whenever the opportunity had presented itself.

How to get back in the orphanage and retrieve his hoard of stolen goods was as always uppermost in Mike's mind. His personal effects had been delivered to The Two Bells Public house the day following his dismissal. But these were not the items he truly needed. In order to move on and live comfortably he had to have his nest egg, or so he thought. Physical hard work was not something he enjoyed. Ordering others around was more to his liking. Mike knew he would need to find work soon, but without a character reference from Joshua Eden this might be difficult.

As he sat nursing his pint of ale, two soldiers entered the pub. They were local boys whom he recognised on sight. They must be home on leave. Mike held up his glass as a toast to the young men as they entered the pub. Now there was an occupation that might just suit him. He knew The Queens' army was actively looking for recruits. Perhaps a spell in the wider world might do him good? Thinking it over, and fuelled by ale, the idea became even better.

He could disappear for a while, miss the trial of James Cooper and return when things had settled down. His nest egg he felt was safely hidden, and would hopefully remain so. With this thought in mind, Mike pushed back his chair and ambled over to the bar. The two soldiers were deep in conversation with the Landlord, enjoying their notoriety in the public house.

'Can I buy you boys a drink?' Mike announced.

The pub fell silent. All eyes and ears were on Mike Unwin. The uncharacteristic gesture had sent a ripple of curiosity throughout the pub. Michael Unwin did nothing for anyone unless there was something in it for himself, were the unspoken words on everyone's lips.

The two young men turned in unison to see who had made the generous offer. Like all in the village of Kingminster they knew The Master, Mike Unwin. The younger of the two soldiers instinctively stepped back putting a distance between himself and The Master of the orphanage.

'It's alright Mike, keep your money, this first one's on me,' announced the landlord.

He had noted the change in atmosphere in his establishment and was keen to keep things friendly and pleasant. Jane, he liked. She was devious, but hard working. The brother was something else. Rumours had reached him of some of Unwin's cruel ways and he had secretly been pleased to hear of his sacking from the orphanage.

'Cheers then lads,' replied Mike as he made his way across the floor back to his solitary table.

There it was again, that horrible feeling of embarrassment and shame. This was becoming too regular. He would have to snap out of it otherwise he would never recover his high standing in the village. Mike could feel the eyes of the regulars upon him as he sat down at his corner table. Perhaps a move away from Kingminster would be for the best. He could then return in a year or so, retrieve his hidden loot and pretend his rise in status was due to the fortune he had made elsewhere. James Cooper's trial was also beginning to play heavily on his mind. Much as he knew he was an accomplished liar, he was no longer relishing the thought of having to give evidence to a crowded courtroom. Joshua Eden's face had become imprinted on his mind. The look of loathing and disgust had surprised and hurt Mike deeply.

He needed to lie low and have the means to live. Draining his glass, Mike headed for the door. A visit to Nottingham town was called for. His associates would have to buy his silence. Setting up James Cooper had been one of his better ideas. However, with his dismissal from the employment of Joshua Eden, a Magistrate might not look with favour on his testimony. Questions could be asked that might tie him literally in knots. His associates needed to know that his silence and disappearance was necessary for them all to avoid the hangman's noose.

Unfortunately, his meeting with his Nottingham associates had not gone well. He had been threatened and told if he valued his life he had better disappear from Nottingham and most definitely from Kingminster. When he had mentioned that he still had the items stolen from Eden Manor, the leader of the gang had told him to dispose of them himself. They were washing their hands of crime for now!

Indignant with fury, Mike considered his options. Perhaps leaving Nottinghamshire for a while might be best. He could always write and ask Jane to retrieve his nest egg, if he felt desperate. For now it might be best to leave them where they were and not arouse suspicion.

As he walked aimlessly around the streets of Nottingham, he passed more soldiers. Perhaps a spell abroad fighting for Queen and Country might be what he needed. He knew he could always count on Jane to worm her way into the orphanage and retrieve his nest egg. He wasn't happy about this arrangement, as he knew she was anything but honest, but he had no choice. Swallowing his pride Mike headed towards the enlistment office.

He would enlist and write to Jane from the safe distance of some far-flung country. There was enough hidden away to keep them both in comfort for the rest of their lives. He knew she would expect that at the very least.

Chapter 29

Inside the orphanage 2019

Lewis and Lupin were filled with dread at the thought of entering the old orphanage. The problem of getting into the ground had been easily solved. During the summer while walking with the dogs in Eden Park, they had come across the back entrance to the building. Lewis had been able to scale the locked gate and peer over at what was once the domestic end of the orphanage. They had agreed to meet up after school, outside the main gates, but without the dogs. They had both brought torches and their mobile phones and Lewis had even taken several pairs of the disposable gloves his mum kept under the kitchen sink. Scouring the surrounding area for anyone who might see them climbing over the back gate, they agreed that it was safe to go. Lewis gave Lupin a leg up, and once she had dropped down on the other side he too climbed over the gate.

The yard was eerily quiet. Standing in one corner stood two stone troughs, similar to those used for animals. But these had not been for the convenience of animals, they were for the inhabitants of the orphanage to use to wash. The black iron pumps stood idle; their work done. Lupin pulled out the bunch of keys and prayed that one of them would open the door which should lead into the kitchen or some such quarter used by the staff. It took several attempts to find the correct key. Each time they tried a new key that did not open the door, they were acutely aware of the clanging noise it made as it hit against another key in the large bundle. Granddad Featherstone was home, and Lupin knew that he had a keen ear for any unusual noise. At last a key turned noisily in the lock and Lupin pushed the door open.

Neither child had expected the building to be quite so cold and dark, but then they remembered that no natural light could enter the ground floor rooms through the boarded-up windows. Added to this was the fading daylight as autumn closed in. Beyond the door they found themselves in what they could only describe as a porch. This led into a large kitchen complete with an enormous pine worktable, and a range cooker even uglier than the one at The Old Rectory. The smell was overwhelming. It was a mixture of decay, mould and damp. Both gasped as they entered the room. Lewis and Lupin stood stock still listening for sounds of movement in the building. As their eyes grew accustomed to the gloom they looked around but saw no signs that someone had been using the kitchen. However, that did not mean that someone hadn't recently been inside the building.

Both found themselves reluctant to talk or even whisper to one another. Lewis pulled out his torch and signalled to Lupin to do the same. Pointing his torch at the floor he gingerly stepped forward with Lupin in his wake. They slowly moved from the kitchen into a long dark corridor which eventually led into the hall. Lewis quickly switched off his torch and Lupin did the same. They were aware that they were now at the main entrance to the building and anyone walking or driving on Kingminster Lane might well spot the torch light through the elaborate fan light over the front door.

Lewis felt a strange feeling of deja vu. He had been here

before, in his dreams to be precise. But now the scene was real and solid. He was no longer a voyeur watching through someone else's eyes, but actually present walking the corridors and floors that Millie and James had walked over a hundred and fifty years ago. A shiver passed through his body, making him want to move on quickly and get the ordeal over sooner rather than later. Instinctively he found himself turning to his right and walking down a corridor parallel to the one they had just used to enter the hallway. Shafts of light streamed through gaps in the window boards making strange patterns on the dusty floor. There it was, the door that Mike Unwin had so carefully opened and locked behind himself in the dream. Lewis hesitated as he reached for the handle. He was uncomfortable about opening this particular door. Millie had left The Master to enter the room alone. He did not know what he might find on the other side of the door. They had turned off their torches by now as their eyes had grown accustomed to the gloomy semi-darkness of the ground floor rooms.

'This was the room that Mike Unwin went into in my dream, I'm sure it's important in some way,' he whispered over his shoulder to Lupin who now stood behind him in the narrow corridor.

The door opened into what looked like a small sitting room. The furniture had all been removed, apart from an old chair which stood forlorn and unused by the small fireplace. A second door led off this room into what would have been The Master's bedroom. The frame of the single iron bed still stood on the bare floorboards. In the corner of the room was a built-in cupboard, the door now hanging off its hinges. Looking inside they found it contained nothing. It had probably been Mike Unwin's closet. The floorboards creaked loudly as they edged their way out of The Master's private quarters and back into the hall.

Several closed doors led off the hallway. Lewis and Lupin tentatively opened each and stepped inside. The building had been stripped of most of its furniture, and in the majority of the rooms all that remained was the original cast iron fireplace and the odd table or chair. Lewis tried to imagine himself sitting on one side of the large rough pine table in what must have been the dining room cum work room. An image of Oliver Twist came into his head and he smiled to himself at the thought of asking for more!

'What's the joke?' asked Lupin with a frown on her face. She could see nothing worth smiling or laughing about in this heartless place.

Lewis explained, but still she did not see the joke.

'Come on, we're meant to be looking for clues, not re-enacting a Victorian story!' she hissed as she pulled his arm to guide him out of the room.

'Millie's letter said George had found the necklace outside Mr Eden's study window. Let's find the study. It might help us get a better understanding of what happened that night,' whispered Lewis.

Carefully closing the door, they walked across the hall. One door opened into what must once have been a broom cupboard; a small dark cramped space, which contained nothing more than mice droppings, cobwebs and spiders. Directly across the hall from the cupboard they found themselves in a very different style of room.

Until now all the rooms they had entered had been soulless, drab and functional. No frills or comforts had graced these rooms. The room they now stepped into was spacious, with a picture rail complemented by ornate coving and a large decorative ceiling rose. The deep skirting board ran from one side of the enormous marble fireplace to the other. Both children had often been told they were tall for their age, but neither one of them was as tall as this fireplace.

'This has got to be it,' whispered Lewis as he once again tried to imagine the room furnished and used back in the Victorian era.

Stepping over to the boarded up sash window Lewis found it easy to imagine himself climbing out of the long window into freedom. But were they ever really free? What had become of Ned, George, Herbert and Robert? At the thought of the boys, and now seeing where they had once lived, Lewis felt a deep sadness for the poor parentless orphans.

Back in the hall they looked up to the top of the wide staircase. It looked sturdy enough, but both had been putting off this moment. What if the person with the torch was still upstairs, lying in wait for them? Lupin pulled Lewis towards the narrow corridor that led to The Master's rooms and whispered that they needed to have their phones at the ready in case of an emergency. If anyone was still in the building they would have heard them moving about downstairs and could now be waiting for them in one of the upstairs rooms.

Pocketing their torches and pulling out their mobile phones, both noticed that they had no signal. Lewis vaguely remembered his mum had once told him that you could always make an emergency call to the police, fire and ambulance service without a signal. He sincerely hoped that she had been right. The stairs groaned noisily as they unsuccessfully tried their best to tiptoe up to the first floor.

Natural light flooded the first-floor landing and made both children squint after the gloom of the ground floor rooms. At the top of the stairs they both took a moment to listen for any sign of life; all was quiet. The layout of the first floor was fairly simple. At the top of the stairs turning right was a door with a sign which read: 'Boys'. Across the landing was an identical door labelled: 'Girls.'

'Best to start in the boys' dormitory,' suggested Lewis. He was feeling a little more relaxed now they had left the dark gloom of the ground floor. Natural light streamed in through the dirty windows giving Lewis and Lupin a modicum of confidence.

Pushing open the door marked 'Boys' they entered the room. It was a large dormitory with long sash windows on one side. Lewis noted that these were the windows that looked out towards The Old Rectory where he had spotted the torch light previously. In what would have once been neat rows stood the rusting iron beds. They had been stripped of their mattresses but apart from that it was easy for the two children to imagine the boys sleeping in this room. There was nothing homely or comforting about it. Like the rooms on the ground floor it was purely functional.

'I wonder which one was James's bed,' whispered Lupin.

'We'll never know,' added Lewis. 'What we need to find out is what the people with the torches were looking for.'

Apart from age-old dust, grime and the old beds the room appeared to contain very little. Several of the floorboards looked as though they had been lifted recently. The children wondered whether Addbridge Construction had done this when they had purchased the building. Whoever had removed them hadn't made a good job of relaying them. Several times both children had tripped on a raised board, and in one instance one had snapped in two with the ease of a wafer biscuit. The old joists creaked with age as Lewis and Lupin walked around the room. In the far corner was a wooden stand with hooks above it. Lewis momentarily imagined himself standing at a bowl washing, then reaching for a towel, or cloth from the hook to dry himself.

'There's nothing in here,' said Lupin. 'Let's go and look in the girls' dormitory.'

Closing the door behind them, they walked across the landing to the door marked 'Girls'. Inside was an identical room to the boys' dormitory. The only difference was that this room looked as though it had not been touched in years. No floorboards had been removed and the beds still stood to attention in neat rows.

'Whoever is searching the place isn't interested in the girls' dormitory, I wonder why not?' muttered Lewis.

Another flight of stairs led up to the attic. The rooms were cramped and looked more like individual prison cells. The dust on the stairs and floors showed signs of footsteps. In each room someone had pulled up the floorboards and not bothered to replace them correctly

'I don't think we are going to find out any more about our torch men from here, let's get out of here and put the keys back before your Gran or Granddad notice they're missing,' said Lewis as he headed for the stairs. Lupin followed and leaving by the back door they quietly closed and locked it, before climbing over the gate onto the dirt track.

Chapter 30

The jewels are returned 2019

Back in the warmth of the Featherstones' kitchen Lupin hung the bunch of keys back on their peg beside the dresser. She then phoned her mum and asked if she could meet her at Lewis's house, explaining that they had something important to tell them. Saying a hasty goodbye to her grandparents, Lupin and Lewis, fired up with adrenaline, ran down the Lane to The Old Rectory. Racing upstairs to the attic room Lewis retrieved the carrier bag from the fireplace and went downstairs in search of his mother.

Lewis's mum was busy painting the dining room, and looked up at the two flushed children with a quizzical frown.

'What's up? Aren't the two of you doing your homework together at Lupin's grandparents?' she asked.

'Lupin's mum and dad should hopefully be here soon, we've something to show you,' said Lewis. 'And we're going to have to go to the police,' he added in order to gain his mother's full attention.

Putting down her roller she stood eyeing the two young people waiting for whatever revelation was about to come next. Lewis had been acting strangely all summer, but she had put this down to the divorce and the move.

'Why will WE have to go to the police Lewis?' she asked,

emphasising the word 'we'.

'Mrs Henry, we've done nothing wrong but it's what we or I mean Truffle found,' said Lupin, trying to lighten the atmosphere which had become distinctly icy.

At that moment the front doorbell rang. Hurrying to the door Lewis let in the confused and worried Andersons.

At first the atmosphere was tense. But the parents relented when they heard what the little pup had found in the derelict barn. At the police station they told how Truffle had somehow found her way into the derelict barns and had become entangled in the rotting pouch and necklace. They then went on to mention the lights Lewis had seen in the empty orphanage, but the police didn't seem particularly interested in this. After making their statements they left the police station and returned to their respective homes. They both had school the next day and that took precedence over all else as far as the parents were concerned.

That night Lewis's head had barely hit the pillow when Millie appeared. She was crying and asking him to come with her. Once more he dreamt of the orphanage. They were outside The Master's rooms, Millie seemed afraid to enter the room. Suddenly the door opened, and Mike Unwin stepped out into the passageway, turned and locked the door behind him. Millie followed him into the large dining room/workroom. The children worked silently, glancing up at the man they feared as he passed through the room. In the back yard, The Master's personality took on a dramatic change. Spying a group of teenage boys, he wandered over to them and whispered something into the ear of a wiry red-haired boy. The boy smiled to himself and winked at the others. During this exchange Mike Unwin's eyes darted to and fro to make sure they were not overheard. Turning from the group he went back into the building, and after inspecting the work of a number of girls in the kitchen he headed back to his rooms. There the dream ended, and Lewis woke with his head ringing with the sound of Millie's voice urging him to search.

By now Lewis was in no doubt that Millie wanted him to search Mike Unwin's former rooms. But what he was looking for he had no idea. Lewis knew that the Eden family would soon be given their ancestors' jewels and hopefully that would be enough proof of James's innocence. Although something inside told him it would not be so simple. For over 150 years James Cooper had been branded a thief. Why would anyone apart from himself, Lupin and Millie wish to clear his name now?

Chapter 31

Headline News 2019

Life for Lewis, Lupin and Truffle continued without much disruption, Millie was silent. They attended school as normal and both had had a visit from the police to take further statements. They had also had to accompany the police up to the barn where the ruby and diamond pendant and matching earrings had been found. They had been informed by the police that the pouch containing the jewels had probably been hidden in an old birds' nest on the rafters. Over time it had fallen to the ground and had simply lain undiscovered, until Truffle had found her way into the barn. A thorough search had been made of all the derelict barns but nothing of interest had come to light.

Several weeks had passed and neither Lewis nor Lupin felt any closer to clearing James's name. When the police had visited Lewis at home he had made the decision to mention James's name, and ask if it would now be cleared, as part of the stolen jewellery from 1860 had been found. He was angry and upset to be told that the case against James Cooper had no bearing on their find and had been closed in 1860, following his trial and conviction. Nothing had changed. Lewis found himself becoming more and more frustrated at the lack of interest from anyone in their attempt to clear the name of the Victorian orphan. The final straw came in the form of an invitation to Eden Manor for afternoon tea on the following Saturday. Both his mother and Lupin's parents were over the moon at the invitation, which even included Truffle.

Discussing the tea party Lewis and Lupin decided they had nothing to lose if they told the Edens the full story, including the involvement of Millie. So far no one had taken a jot of notice of their reports of an intruder in the empty orphanage. On several occasions since Truffle had found the missing pendant and earrings, Lewis had seen the now familiar torch light glinting in the first and second floor windows of the orphanage. He had taken pictures using his phone. They were evidence as he saw it. His mum and the police didn't seem to agree, and had suggested that it was someone connected to Addbridge Construction. Knowing when to be silent Lewis had become withdrawn. He was unbelievably angry with his mother; whose major concern was what she would wear to the tea party! Lupin's parents were no better, while her grandparents were a little put out at not being included in the invitation to the grand Manor House.

At last the great day came around. Scrubbed and smartly dressed Lewis waited by Mr Anderson's impressive family car with Truffle at his feet sniffing the nearest tyre. She too had had to undergo extra special preparation. The pup had been taken to a local dog groomer and had been bathed, clipped and perfumed in readiness for the big outing. All for the sake of drinking a bowl of water in a big house! Standing on the pavement outside his home Lewis watched with indifference as his mother made a great fuss of getting into the back of the car with Sally Anderson and Lupin. She sat bolt upright like a doll, not wanting to crease her new dress. Sally Anderson had the hem of her dress folded over her arm, in an attempt to keep it crease free! The adults were behaving like a group of excited children on an outing.

Despite his visible annoyance at his mother's behaviour Lewis did enjoy the tour of the Manor House. It was a truly beautiful and comfortable home, regardless of its size. The Edens were effusive with their gratitude and delight at the restoration of their ancestor's precious necklace and earrings. The children were repeatedly questioned on their 'chance' find of the jewels.

During the conversation Lewis and Lupin had used the opportunity to ask Mr and Mrs Eden whether they would now help them clear James Cooper's name, and possibly find out what had happened to him after his trial. On this score they were to be disappointed. They had hit a stone wall. At the mention of Millie and her letter Lewis and Lupin were horrified to hear that the family still believed that James was guilty, along with the four runaway boys and other unknown partners in crime. They insisted that Truffle's find was only a small part of the many valuable items that had been stolen on that fateful night in 1860. The Edens were adamant that they would have no part in digging up the past, but were nonetheless extremely grateful to Truffle, Lupin and Lewis, and even tried to present them with a cheque for £5,000.00 as a mark of their gratitude.

Both children had refused the money and stated in no uncertain terms that what they wanted was their help in finding out what had happened to James Cooper and to clear his name. After much gushing from the parents, the dreadful tea party was over. Asking to be excused Lewis and Lupin decided to walk home. Neither could bear another minute in the company of their fawning parents.

Life carried on much as before. Lewis felt Millie's presence on a regular basis, it was as if she too was disappointed in the actions of the present-day Eden family, his mother and Lupin's parents. He and Lupin were alone in their quest to clear the name of James Cooper. Millie quietly continued to urge them on. However, help was to come from quite a different quarter.

To both children's surprise their parents were approached by the local BBC TV station to ask if they, along with Truffle, would like to appear on television to talk about their remarkable discovery. After discussing it with their parents and one another they agreed. Both felt that the publicity might just flush out the torch men. This in turn might lead them to the rest of the stolen jewellery. By now Millie was becoming something of a nuisance to Lewis. Almost every night she had appeared in his dreams, always taking him into the old orphanage. She was not giving up, which meant that Lewis and Lupin felt honour bound to help the Victorian servant girl. The Nottingham Evening Post had featured a piece on the restoration of valuable jewels to one of Nottinghamshire's leading families. While at school the two young people found themselves heroes. Everyone was interested in how a dog had found priceless valuable jewels which had lain hidden for over 150 years.

In all of the drama one player was not happy, and that was Millie. Their find had only succeeded in urging her on to prove James's innocence. Lewis and Lupin both felt the same way, but where were the rest of the jewels? The police had conducted a thorough search of the barns and found nothing. They had informed the parents that unless they had concrete evidence of wrongdoing in the orphanage they could not enter the building and search it. So there it was left, with Millie constantly interrupting Lewis's sleep urging him to search in the empty orphanage.

It was now several weeks since the discovery and their TV appearance. Notwithstanding Millie's constant presence things had settled down considerably. One morning out of the blue a letter addressed to Lewis dropped through the letterbox.

It was from an Andrew Cooper in Western Australia. Lewis was astounded to read that this was the great great great grandson of James Cooper. He had seen the news story on Australian TV and felt compelled to contact Lewis, Lupin and Truffle. The letter explained that his great, great, great grandfather had been sentenced to 7 years transportation to Australia in September 1860. James had survived the 122 days gruelling journey from Chatham Docks to Australia. He had worked off his sentence as a labourer. At the end of the sentence he had not the financial means to return to England. He had missed his little sister Millie and had written several times to her at The Rectory, but he had never received a reply. James, saddened by Millie's silence, had settled in Australia, and married and had had five children who in turn had gone on to producing more of their own.

Lewis phoned Lupin immediately he had read the letter. Both felt a mixture of emotions as Lewis read the letter over the phone. He had felt no shame at crying as he read aloud each deeply meaningful and saddening word. A life had been stolen and another lost to a broken heart. He had called to Millie as he read the letter from her great, great, great nephew, and had silently prayed that she had heard him and could now rest.

On the Sunday, Lewis and his mother had been invited to the Featherstones' for lunch. Lewis's mum and Sally Anderson had become firm friends, and it was a family tradition that Grandma Featherstone always cooked the Sunday lunch. While seated around the large kitchen table Lewis found himself staring across the room at the row of keys hanging from pegs, next to the cluttered dresser. He knew where to find the keys to the orphanage, and several times he wondered if anyone would miss them if he were to 'borrow' them.

The conversation, as it so often did, turned to the latest

developments from Addbridge Construction. It appeared that the planning application had been passed, and work would soon be starting in earnest on the project. On hearing this Lewis made the decision to take the keys when no one was looking and have one final look around the building before it was too late. He had no difficulty in lifting the keys from their peg and slipping them into his pocket. Lupin had left at the same time with her parents, so he knew that she would not notice the empty peg. He sincerely hoped that neither of the Featherstones would notice the missing keys, or that they would get a call on Monday morning asking them to let someone into the orphanage.

That night Lewis found himself dreaming of Mike Unwin's room. In his dream it was the same room he and Lupin had entered weeks ago. He found himself standing in the middle of the bedroom reaching out and touching the walls. He woke in a sweat, wondering what the significance of the dream was. This was not Millie guiding him, so what did it all mean? He would soon find out, as he planned to skip school and take another look in the orphanage. Lewis had agonised over telling Lupin of his plans, but decided it might be better if only he played truant from school. He felt he was doing her a favour by not asking her to accompany him.

On the Monday morning Lewis breakfasted as normal. Kissing his mum and Truffle goodbye, he picked up his school bag and left the house. At the bottom of Church Lane he turned and doubled back on himself. Walking quickly, he hunched his shoulders as he hurried past his home and the church and turned into Eden Park. At the back entrance to the orphanage he swiftly climbed over the gate, landing on the other side without a sound. From his bag he took out his torch which he then transferred to his pocket. Checking his mobile phone he noted a text message from Lupin, asking why he wasn't at the bus stop. He quickly fired off a text telling her he was ill and would not be in school that day. He hoped that the school would not contact his mother to ask why he had not turned up, but felt that apart from trying to impersonate his mum, he would have to hope that his absence would not be questioned immediately. He could tell the truth later.

Inside the orphanage it didn't take Lewis long to find Mike Unwin's rooms. Millie had shown him where he needed to search. Lifting the floorboards had proved tricky at first; eventually he had managed to remove several of the swollen boards. He gasped at what he saw hidden in the void. What he had thought was a handkerchief was in fact another cotton pouch identical to the old torn pouch Truffle had found in the barn. There were several of them, all packed in close together in the cramped space, and all looked as if they were full. Lewis instinctively knew what he would find in the pouches, the haul from Eden Manor. But there was more. As he lifted out each pouch below it was another and another. The space under the floorboards was crammed full of treasure. Opening one of the pouches he stared with amazement at enough signet rings to adorn the hands of at least two people. Other pouches contained necklaces, brooches, rings, bracelets and earrings. Some contained ornate silver candle holders and snuff boxes. Lewis wondered how much of what he was looking at had come from Eden Manor. Not wanting to linger for a minute longer he quickly stuffed the pouches into his school bag. He decided against replacing the floorboards; the police would want to take a look at where he had unearthed the latest windfall. As he was stuffing the last pouch into his bag, he smiled to himself. James was innocent, without a shadow of a doubt. The true criminal had to have been Mike Unwin. He now had the proof!

He, Lewis Henry, Lupin Anderson and Truffle would clear

James's name, of that he was sure. How they would do it was another matter, but he knew it could be done. He had seen it on the news and the internet. As he closed the zip on his school bag, something else caught his eye. Once more he bent down to reach into the space under the floorboard and pulled out a shoe. A girl's shoe to be precise, very old and now very dirty. Even in its present state Lewis could appreciate that this was once a shoe worn by a well-to-do child. So what was it doing hidden under the floorboards?

Pulling it free Lewis noticed that something had been pushed into its toe. Wrapped in a small piece of lace was a locket. Thinking no more of this, he quickly stuffed the shoe and its contents into his bag and got up to leave the room. He would worry about the significance of the shoe later, it might be of no consequence. The sound of a door opening froze Lewis to the spot. Someone had entered the building. He had deliberated with himself whether or not to lock himself in the building and had decided against it, thinking he was safe. Neither he nor Lupin and the Featherstones had heard or seen any disturbance since they had taken the diamond and ruby pendant and earrings to the police. Whoever had been searching had given up, or so they had thought. Who could it be? Addbridge Construction were not scheduled to send anyone to the building, he had confirmed that yesterday.

'Tell me again what the letter said?' came a rough gravelly voice from the hallway.

'It said he had treasures worth a fortune in his room at the orphanage,' another voice replied.

'I don't get it, we've searched all the staff rooms and found nothing. I still think it's in here. We're probably searching in the wrong place. As far as I know this dump has been shut up for over a hundred years and more,' replied the man with the gravelly voice.

Lewis instinctively knew that these were the men who had been searching the orphanage. So they were looking for treasure. He had just found it! His heart raced, if they found him now his school bag would be searched. His discovery and proof of James's innocence would disappear along with the two men. Who would believe him without the proof? He had to hide the bag to ensure no one but Lupin and the police could see its contents. If he were discovered in the orphanage, he could pretend he was just looking round out of idle curiosity. But where would be a suitable hiding place? Thinking quickly Lewis remembered the large fireplace in the grand room that must have been Joshua Eden's study. If he could stay hidden for long enough, he might be able to stuff the bag up the chimney. Footsteps told him they were in the passage outside Mike Unwin's room. Holding his breath and praying that they wouldn't try the door, Lewis stood as still as a statue behind the bedroom door. Trying not to breathe Lewis waited as they opened the door to the sitting room. He fully expecting them to venture further into the room and into the bedroom beyond and find him hiding behind the door. But after a cursory glance around the sitting room they decided it held nothing of interest to them and moved on. Their heavy tread could be heard as they climbed the stairs. He had to move fast and quietly, not an easy task on the unstable and twisted floorboards. He waited until he could hear the men overhead and eased opened the door.

Taking large strides, so as to make as little noise as possible he made it to the sitting room door. From the passageway Lewis had to make his next move as swiftly as possible. He would be exposed once he stepped into the hall; either or both of the men only had to look over the banister to see him. He had to make it across the hall and into the grand study without detection. Fortunately, the hall floor was tiled and there would be no creaking floor boards to give him away. Looking to his right and left, Lewis remembered the broom cupboard. If he couldn't make it out of the building, he might try hiding in there until the men had gone. It was a plan of sorts. Taking a deep breath and striding on his tip toes Lewis crossed the hall and opened the door to the study. Quietly closing the door, he hastened over to the fireplace. Pushing with all his might he managed to shove his school rucksack into the chimney cavity. Age old soot fell into the grate and onto his arms and feet, but he had no time to worry about that. He needed to get out of the building and fast. At the door he again listened for the tread of the men on the upper floor. The voices seemed quieter, that could only mean they had gone further up to the servants' quarters. This was good, thought Lewis; he might not need the shelter of the broom cupboard after all.

Pulling the study door shut Lewis once again cocked his ear to listen for the two men. On hearing nothing he hurried across the hall floor and hoped that they could not hear the pounding of his heart as he made his way across the floor, this time towards the kitchen and back door. He had decided that it was best for him to get out rather than hide in the broom cupboard. He stepped gingerly on the old floorboards in the passage leading to the kitchen.

'Not far now,' he whispered to himself by way of encouragement, and then he felt it.

A grip like a vice around his middle. Lewis tried to struggle free, but he was helpless. His arms were held tight and he could do no more than wriggle and attempt to kick the shins of the man who had picked him up and was now swinging him from side to side as if he were a rag doll.

'Not so fast mate,' said the man as he turned Lewis round to face him.

The face he was looking at had to be the man he had seen in his first week in Kingminster, the man in the white van.

'What you doing in here anyway? Don't you know its private property?' Lewis decided against answering the man immediately. He needed time to think. If he played this right he might just get away.

'I hate school so I thought I would bunk off and have a look around this place,' he replied after a whole host of ideas and possibilities had coursed through his head.

White Van man considered Lewis's remarks and smiled. 'School not your thing then?' he asked, smiling.

His grip around Lewis's middle had loosened, but Lewis knew that he would never be able to outrun someone who looked as though marathon running was something he did on a regular basis... The man had to be over 6ft 3in at least.

'How'd you get in?' he asked.

Now Lewis had been dreading this question. He didn't want to cause any trouble for the Featherstones by saying he had taken their key, neither did he think that a direct lie would help. If he were searched the man would find the bunch of keys in his trousers pocket. He needed time to think. The man's expression had changed from smiling to a scowl.

'Who else is with you?' he asked, tightening his grip on Lewis and once again lifting him off his feet.

'No one, I told you I bunked off school,' replied Lewis.

If the man's skull had been transparent Lewis could have sworn he could see his brain trying hard to compute the information he had been given. At that moment the door was pushed open by another man. He was the total opposite of White Van man in physique. While one was tall and lean, the other looked as if the gym was his place of worship, he had biceps on his biceps.

'What the hell is going on here Gary?' he exclaimed as he took in the scene of Lewis dangling from White Van man's arms.

'Who's this then? And what's he doing here?'

'Says he's skipped school and broke in here for somethin' to do,' replied White Van man.

For what seemed like hours the two men stood and stared at Lewis. Eventually White Van man had put him down and released him from his vice like grip. Lewis looked from one man to the other, both were now thinking hard. He knew they were trying to decide what to do next. Changing tack, Bicep Man grabbed Lewis and pushed him along the corridor back into the hall. He then proceeded to drag him upstairs and threw him onto the floor of the boys' dormitory. His companion had followed, and was now mumbling to himself, Lewis found it hard to fully understand what he was saying, but it didn't sound good.

"He's seen our faces, he can identify us, and whoops mate I've told him your name!' snapped Bicep Man.

'I'm not doing 'owt bad. I told you before. He's only a kid. Let's get out of here, there's nothing here anyway. If there was we'd have found it by now,'mumbled White Van Man AKA Gary.

Both men stood for a moment thinking. Lewis lay on the floor praying that they would see sense and allow him to leave. Somehow he didn't think so, from the expression on Bicep Man's face.

'Tie him up and let's go,' ordered Bicep Man, pulling out his mobile phone and frowning. Walking from the room he dialled a number and listened intently to what must have been a voice mail message.

'Come on, leave him. But listen to me kid, you've not seen us, and you've been in here alone, do you understand me?' He said with menace. Lewis nodded his head, silently praying that they would now leave the building.

'Get on with it you idiot, tie him up!' shouted Bicep Man as he strode from the room, pointing furiously at Lewis as if to emphasise who needed to be tied up. Whatever news he had received on his phone had hastened his need to leave the building quickly.

Gary looked around for something to use to tie Lewis up with. Apart from the iron bedframes there was nothing. To Lewis's surprise he winked at him and then added in a loud voice.

'That's got ya you little sod, see if you can get out of that!'

Shrugging his shoulders he closed the door, Lewis heard his heavy tread as he descended the stairs in search of his companion. In a state of shock and relief Lewis lay on the dormitory floor. He dared not move in case Bicep Man realised that he had not been tied up. After several minutes of listening intently he cautiously got up from the floor and crept over to the window. Through the smeared glass he could see nothing of any use to himself. They had probably parked the van further up the lane, so there was no way of knowing whether they had left or not. He decided to take a chance and headed for the door. Again the rotten floorboards creaked with the strain of his weight. He was just about to turn the door handle when he felt the floor beneath his feet move. Lewis felt himself falling.

It was dark when he came to. His left leg screamed with pain. Each rasping breath caused him agonizing pain. His leg had to be broken, and his head felt as if he had been hit with a church bell. Trying to turn to a chink of light Lewis realised that he was no longer in the boys' dormitory. The darkness was because he had fallen into one of the ground floor rooms. Pain shot through his leg as he tried to reach into his pocket for his mobile phone. Each movement made him gag. At last he had the phone in his hand. Pressing the 'on' button Lewis almost wept when he saw that the battery was flat. Why, oh why, hadn't he planned this better and charged his phone, and left a message for Lupin or a note for his mother?

It was too late to cry over what he hadn't done. Sweat was pouring off his forehead. Yet he found himself shivering. Lewis knew he needed help and soon. Perhaps if he called out Lupin's grandparents might hear him and realise that someone was in the building. Lewis began to shout, but each effort cut through his body like a knife and increased the pounding in his head. He had no idea which of the downstairs rooms he was in. But he did know that the boys' dormitory had been on the opposite side of the building to the Featherstones' house. On this side of the building there was only garden and fields. In fact the nearest building would be one of the houses on Church Lane, some quarter of a mile away!

Remembering what his mother had said about making a call to the emergency services Lewis picked up his mobile phone from the floor and tried to dial 999.There was no response: the battery was well and truly dead. Either that or there was no signal through the solid Victorian walls, or the phone had broken when he had fallen through the floor. The effort alone of reaching for the phone and pressing the buttons, had brought on another wave of nausea. His head hurt, as did his shoulder and back. Looking towards the window he tried to gauge the time of day. He had no idea how long he had been unconscious. All he could now pray for, was that his mum would wonder why he hadn't come home from school on the bus as normal, and hopefully ask Lupin if she knew where he might be. He felt confident that Lupin wouldn't let him down. She would work out where he had gone and bring help. Several times he had found himself almost drifting into a welcoming sleep. Sleep would numb the pain, and the pain was becoming unbearable.

Chapter 32

Truffle and Lupin to the rescue 2019

Lupin had missed the company of Lewis at school. Several times she had wondered what had made him ill. He had seemed perfectly fine yesterday, overeating her grandma's puddings. Perhaps that was it, her gran had finally poisoned someone with her cooking! Laughing to herself she sent him yet another text asking if her gran had given him food poisoning. Surely he would see the joke and reply. Thinking him to be very ill, she considered whether she should call in on him that evening or leave it until tomorrow. She decided to leave him to contact her when he was feeling better and put him out of her mind.

She had been watching TV when her mother came into the lounge and asked if she knew where Lewis was. The question immediately sounded warning bells in her head. Where could he be if he were not at home? It was after seven and he had not gone to school!

Lewis's mum came into the lounge looking as if she had been crying. She explained that he had left for school as normal and she had not become concerned until it had grown dark and he had not answered any of her text messages or phone calls.

'I expect his phone is dead. He never remembers to charge it fully, but where can he be?' she said as she reached for another tissue.

Picking up her own mobile phone Lupin also tried to phone Lewis. The phone went straight to voice mail, a clear sign that the battery was flat. Thinking hard Lupin tried to remember if he had said anything more about his dreams and the old orphanage. Nothing came to mind, and she didn't wish to even start to try to explain who and what Millie was. It had been bad enough at the Edens with looks of disbelief passing from face to face.

'Mum can you drive me over to Gran's please?'

An idea had come to her. Desperate to try anything, Lewis's mum said that she would drive Lupin and bring her back later, but Sally Anderson, seeing the distress on her new friend's face said that she would meet Lewis's mum over at her parents' house.

Mr Featherstone opened the door to three worried faces. In a matter of seconds Lewis's mum had explained the reason for her distress and asked them if they had any idea where Lewis might be. In the meantime, Lupin had gone into the kitchen to look for the keys to the orphanage. She felt pretty certain that she would find them gone, and she had guessed correctly. In that case she would go and find him. All being well the parents would be none the wiser. He probably was still looking for clues to prove James's innocence. Walking into the hall she wondered what excuse she could use to get out of the house. It was now dark outside. Her mother and grandparents wouldn't let her wander off by herself; particularly as her best friend was missing. Looking through the window she noted that Mrs Henry had brought Truffle with her. The little dog had her nose up at the half open window sniffing the night air.

'Truffle looks like she needs to go to the toilet and have a little walk. Shall I take her now?' she suggested, trying not to make eye contact with any of the adults.

Opening the car door Lupin led Truffle into the house. Finding a lead, she attached it to the dog's collar and took her into the back garden. Looking up at the orphanage she saw no sign of life. She was sure Lewis was in there, where else could he be? He knew few people in the village. Slipping through the back gate Lupin ran with the excited dog around to the front of her grandparents' house. It would have saved her a great deal of time if she had been able to put a ladder up against the connecting wall and climb over into the orphanage grounds from their garden. But too many questions would have needed answers before that took place. If indeed she were allowed to do such a thing!

Lupin held Truffle's lead tightly as she ran down the lane, passing Lewis's house and on into Eden Park, much to the confusion of Truffle, who pulled and whined at her gate, obviously expecting to go inside. Lupin had picked up a torch as she had left her grandparents' house. She used it now to negotiate her way into the unlit park. Reaching the back gate of the orphanage she questioned her judgement in bringing the dog. She could just about make it over the gate, but she wouldn't be able to carry the dog over it. There was no time to turn back and nowhere for her to tie the dog. She guessed that Truffle might run off and find her way home, but she could not take that risk.

Holding the lead firmly she decided to call to Lewis. She reasoned if he was in the building he would hear her and come out. After calling his name several time with Truffle added her voice to this new game. Lupin heard a faint knocking sound from within the building. Lewis or someone was in there. She called again and put her ear to the gate. There it was again. Maybe he had tripped on one of the rotten floorboards and was hurt. Truffle's enthusiastic barking and tail wagging convinced her that the noise must be being made by Lewis. The little dog seemed to have recognised her Master's presence! She was now frantically scratching at the gate, anxious to get inside.

With her heart in her mouth Lupin took out her phone and phoned her mother. After numerous interruptions she was eventually able to explain that she thought Lewis was in the empty orphanage and possibly hurt. In a matter of minutes Lewis's mum's voice could be heard calling to her son from the Featherstones' garden. Looking towards the wall which linked the orphanage to her grandparents' house Lupin could just make out the shape of a figure. Lewis's mum must have been standing on the top of a ladder.

Shouting over to Mrs Henry, Lupin explained that she thought Lewis had gone into the building through the back entrance. After what seemed like hours, with Truffle pulling one way and then another, she heard the sound of someone landing on the ground, followed by a string of swear words! It was her mum, who had jumped over the adjoining wall and was on the other side of the gate. Within minutes she heard more swearing as Lewis's mum landed in the orphanage back yard. Sounds of scraping resulted in the back gate being unbolted and Mrs Henry standing dishevelled and anxious staring at Lupin. Saying nothing she took the lead from Lupin and stood holding the excited dog. Her own mother had muttered that they would talk about this later.

'This is turning into a family picnic,' thought Lupin. 'All this fuss! I'll kill him if I'm grounded after this!'

Mrs Anderson pushed open the back door to the orphanage and stepped inside. She put out her hand for Lupin to pass her the torch, which she did.

'Which way?' she asked.

'Give me the torch and follow me,' Lupin replied as she again called Lewis's name.

The tapping was coming from the work room. Leading the

way down the corridor Lupin followed the sound and pushed open the door. Lewis was lying on the dining room floor; his leg looked like that of a puppet that had been tossed into the corner. He was pale and obviously in a great deal of pain. Three mobile phones were pulled out in unison.

'Truffle!' whispered Lewis and then he fainted.

Chapter 33

All is well in Kingminster Village 2019

Lewis had sustained a broken leg, concussion, and bruising, but otherwise he was in remarkably good shape considering he had fallen through a ceiling. When he had eventually come round, his mother's face told him that he had a lot of explaining to do, but for now she was content to wait until he was stronger before starting her interrogation. Lupin was not so fortunate. Her parents and grandparents had repeatedly questioned her on why Lewis had been in the empty building in the first place, and how many times had she been inside the building? Did she know it was wrong, and that it was trespassing?

After an overnight stay in hospital Lewis was allowed home. As they drove into Church Lane Lewis was horrified to see his dad's car parked outside the house. He struggled to use the crutches, preferring to lean his weight against his mother. He hoped to put off the inevitable interrogation he knew was coming from both his parents. Once inside the house Lewis braced himself for the onslaught of questions. He was relieved to find that for now they were more concerned with his health than what he had been doing in the old orphanage.

The night spent in hospital had given him a time to think. He desperately needed to speak to Lupin, and preferably, before he told the police and the parents about the men, and more importantly what he had found. He was now more than ever convinced than James Cooper had been wronged. An innocent boy had lost his only family member and possibly his life, simply because he was poor and had had no one to speak up for him. By the evening Lewis was bored and longed to speak to Lupin. He knew she would be home from school by now. Steeling himself, he asked his mum if he could use her phone to call Lupin. His mum looked annoyed, and grudgingly handed Lewis her phone. Lewis hoped that Lupin would not be put off answering the phone when she saw that the caller was Mrs Henry.

After two rings a timid voice answered. It soon changed when she realised who she was talking to. Lewis quickly explained what had transpired on the Monday morning, and several times apologised for not telling her his plans for that day. They both agreed that Lewis needed to tell the police about the contents of his school bag and where to find it. They could not take the chance that the bag would remain hidden for much longer. The two men might go back into the orphanage at any time and discover it. The two children were now totally convinced of James's innocence and that Mike Unwin was The Mastermind behind the robbery at Eden Manor over 150 years ago.

'Do you think the police will see it that way though?' questioned Lupin. She somehow felt that as the police, and indeed, all in power had been so sure of James's guilt, would they now wish to admit that they had got it wrong all those years ago?

'Will his name be cleared?' asked Lewis, although he knew that he intended to fight tooth and nail to ensure that it was.

'We'll have to wait and see, but I think it wouldn't do any harm to let his Australian family know what we've uncovered. They can help with any fight to clear his name,' replied Lupin.

'Lewis, do you think Millie knows?' she added.

Lewis smiled. He knew that Millie knew. When his mum had helped him into bed, his bedroom curtains had fluttered and a sense of warmth and peace had filled the room. The natural light had seemed much brighter. Yes, Millie knew, and he reckoned she was pretty happy. But Lewis knew it was not over yet. Placing the mobile phone on the bedside table he called for his parents and braced himself. They must have been hovering around on the landing outside his bedroom door as, much to his annoyance, they appeared immediately.

Once again Lewis told his story, and his reasons for skipping school in order to search the orphanage. He carefully omitted any mention of Millie. Dad was visibly angry and turned to his mum with a cruel look on his face. The unspoken words hit Lewis hard. His dad blamed his mum, and probably would try to ban Lewis from being friends with Lupin, even though she had saved his life. The last thing Lewis remembered was hearing his mother on the phone calling the police. Lewis had slipped into a deep sleep.

The next morning he was woken by his mother who informed him that the police had arrived to take yet another statement from him. After endless questioning and much raising of eyebrows the police finally left. Later that evening mum told him that they had rung to say they had searched the orphanage and found his school bag and its contents. Lewis had given them a description of the two men and had even tried to put in a good word for Gary the man in the white van for not tying him up.On the following Monday morning Lewis returned to school. He still struggled with the crutches but was glad to be out of the house. He had heard his parents arguing on the Tuesday evening after he had told them his tale of the orphanage and finding the jewellery. Dad had left shortly after that, promising to keep in touch more regularly once he was back in London. It was now time for Lewis to contact James's family in Australia.

Lewis and Lupin wrote, and re-wrote, the email several times. They felt it necessary to inform Andrew Cooper of all the events that had led up to Lewis finding the hidden jewellery. Within hours Lewis had received a reply. Andrew Cooper was overwhelmed with thanks and joy. He had apparently contacted his local MP and a campaign had been started to posthumously clear James's name. He urged Lewis to also contact his own MP and suggested they spread the word via the internet. "How many other poor souls had been wrongfully transported for crimes they had not committed?" he had added. Millie had gone, Lewis was sure of it. This in itself had made Lewis feel sad, he had become fond of the ghost girl. But he knew she could now rest in peace; her precious brother's name would be cleared.

It was a Saturday morning. Several months had elapsed since the police had searched the orphanage. There had been no news on the capture of the two men, and Lewis had given up any hope of them ever being found. As he sat at his laptop looking out of the bedroom window, he tried to make sense of the events that had taken place in this small supposedly sleepy village. He was brought back to reality by his mother calling him in her 'posh' high pitched voice, the one that she only used when she wished to impress someone. Truffle greeted him at the bottom of the stairs with her now customary kangaroo jumps. The reason for the 'posh voice' was a visit from Mrs Eden. Mum was all a-flutter, acting like she was a serving wench from the past. Lewis cringed as he watched her offering the woman virtually everything they had in the pantry.

Guessing that Mrs Eden had something important to say. Lewis asked if she would wait for him to call Lupin. He explained that they had worked together as a team along with

Truffle, and it was only fair that she was included in any further conversations regarding the old orphanage and its contents. He had been annoyed that the police had questioned them separately and had seemed to doubt much of their story. But they had both done their best not to mention Millie, explaining that Lewis had found the newspaper while exploring his new home, while Truffle had scratched at the wall in the coal house and revealed the letter. These two items, and the lights they had seen in the upstairs windows of the orphanage had been the catalyst for their investigation.

With Lupin and Truffle present, Mrs Eden explained that a large portion of the contents of the cotton pouches had been stolen from her husband's great, great, grandparents in 1860. Other items had subsequently been found to be part of local robberies at around the same time. The police were now trying to trace the owners of several of the items. Mrs Eden expressed her gratitude and when both Lewis and Lupin once again mentioned clearing the name of James Cooper she agreed without hesitation.

'I believe Joshua, my husband's great, great, grandfather would have been proud of you. You know it broke him when he realised that he had been deceived by the orphanage manager. I believe that was why he closed the orphanage so soon after the boy had been transported. He was a good man, with good intentions for the poor, but he put his trust in the wrong people. It's so sad to think of that brother and sister losing each other when so young.'

'Maybe now they can both rest in peace,' muttered Lupin.

'One last thing, my dears. The shoe and locket – where did you find those?' asked Mrs Eden as she leant forward in her chair.

Lewis explained how they also had been pushed into the

space under the floorboards, along with the pouches containing the jewellery.

Mrs Eden seemed to have difficulty digesting this information. She sat bent forward with her head in her hands. Lewis and Lupin were at a loss to know what to do. Truffle, ever playful, put her head in the woman's lap and began to lick her hands. Pushing the puppy away, Mrs Eden looked from Lewis to Lupin and back again.

'I think you need to speak to my husband; he will explain the significance of the two items. The locket and shoe belonged to Annabel's twin sister. She disappeared on a visit to the factory in 1859, presumably abducted. Her nanny pleaded her innocence, claiming she had only turned her back for a minute, but enough time for a toddler to disappear'.

Truffle yelped and Lewis and Lupin grinned as Mrs Eden turned to see who had turned on the light.

Epilogue

What became of George, Ned, Herbert and Robert? Herbert and Robert made it to London and thrived as honest hardworking traders. Life also improved for Ned. A farmer took pity on him, when he found him sleeping rough in his cow shed. He was taken into the family and lived and worked alongside them until old age. George never made the journey to Derby, and never had the opportunity to send a letter to the Eden family. Weak from heat exhaustion, he had fallen asleep in a hedgerow and never woke up.

Millie stayed on at the rectory, much to the annoyance of Agnes. When the Peabody's first child was born, she had been promoted from general housemaid to nanny. Sadly she never received any correspondence from James. She died a year later. Consumed with guilt, Agnes found it hard to remain in employment at the rectory. She left and returned to her family, giving no other explanation than that the position did not suit.

Archibald and Cynthia had a beautiful baby girl, followed by a son two years later. After a succession of unsuitable staff, they eventually made the move from Kingminster to Nottingham.

Jane Unwin married one of the Two Bells regulars and moved from living over the pub into a cottage in the village. Fed up with Mike's moaning in his letters about the heat, flies and the harsh discipline of the army, she stopped opening them.

His letters were placed in a drawer unopened. She planned, when she had the time, that she would eventually get round to reading them. Little did she realise the true content of his final letter.

The Eden family continued to live at Eden Manor, and remained an integral part of Kingminster village.

ACKNOWLEDGEMENTS

I would like to thank my husband Dave, who has had to listen to my ramblings and thoughts as I configured the final story. Added to which he has had to read and re-read several sections of the story as I pieced it all together, and finally the whole book:

Marion Edwards, my friend, for having such patience with me through the many changes and re writes:

All the wonderful family, friends and others who have supported and encouraged me throughout this difficult time in my life:

Last but not least, Ian Edwards, for his stunning cover design for the book, and for putting the whole thing together for publishing.

Printed in Great Britain
by Amazon

43957373R00142